Love is
a time of enchantment:
in it all days are fair and all fields
green. Youth is blest by it,
old age made benign: the eyes of love see
roses blooming in December,
and sunshine through rain. Verily
is the time of true-love
a time of enchantment — and
Oh! how eager is woman
to be bewitched!

DOM

Library at Home Service
Community Services
Hounslow Library, CentreSpace
24 Treaty Centre, High Street
Hounslow TW3 1ES

YOUR COMMUNITY
YOUR SERVICES

0	1	2	3	4	5	6	7	8	9
490	861		3283	704	525	706	3457	858	759
3350	611		9439	784 801	116	686	3188	689	
						346 7927			
3190						630 6			9529
						266			
						6329			

P10-L-2061

✓

KISS OF HOT SUN

Kerry found herself in Sicily helping the once-famous actress Adeline Harcourt run her villa as a guest house. But Kerry soon realises that the Villa Stella d'Oro is no ordinary guest house. Why do people she previously met in Rome start to turn up? And what is Philip Rainsby, whom she had spent one magical evening with, doing here? Kerry loved Philip, but dare she trust him? Almost at once she is caught up in a sinister plot, leading to a life-and-death chase through the wild Sicilian mountains.

Books by Nancy Buckingham
in the Ulverscroft Large Print Series:

THE DARK SUMMER
CLOUD OVER MALVERTON
CALL OF GLENGARRON

NANCY BUCKINGHAM

KISS OF
HOT SUN

Complete and Unabridged

ULVERSCROFT
Leicester

First published in Great Britain in 1969 by
Robert Hale Limited
London

First Large Print Edition
published September 1991

British Library CIP Data

Buckingham, Nancy
   Kiss of hot sun. — Large print ed. —
Ulverscroft large print series: romance
I. Title
823.914 [F]

ISBN 0–7089–2495–6

Published by
F. A. Thorpe (Publishing) Ltd.
Anstey, Leicestershire
Set by Words & Graphics Ltd.
Anstey, Leicestershire
Printed and bound in Great Britain by
T. J. Press (Padstow) Ltd., Padstow, Cornwall

1

THE second time I knew for sure he was looking at me.

Constantly the line of vision between us was blocked. Sweating Italian waiters, trays held high, pushed through the throng of laughing, chitchatting guests. But his eyes ignored these interruptions, and lingered upon me.

Again I looked away quickly, strangely disturbed by that intent, penetrating, and very personal stare.

It shouldn't have been all that earth-shattering for a man to be looking me over; especially not in Rome, and in the month of May! Just five days here had taught me not to give men so much as a milligram of encouragement.

But this man wasn't an Italian, he was British. I knew that from his clothes, his haircut, everything about him. And he was looking at me as if no one else in that huge, glittering salon existed. Only me.

I tried hard to engross myself in the

conversation of the group I was for the moment attached to. It was the usual party small talk of an international set — banal mediocrities processed by alcohol into gems of wit.

It didn't hold my attention. I glanced — casually, I hoped — across to the high graceful windows thrown open to a balcony and the cool night air.

He was no longer there! Not beside the window. Not anywhere that I could see.

I had a ridiculous sense of disappointment. Irritably, I began to wonder how I could detach myself from my unappealing companions.

It was Monica who saved me. She came tripping over excitedly, cocktail glass held before her as a pathfinder. Close on her heels was a middle-aged man, quietly dressed; and as I guessed before he so much as opened his mouth, quietly spoken too.

"Kerry, my pet," Monica gushed. "I want you to meet my very dear friend, Sam Tracy."

"I sure am glad to know you, Miss Lyndon." The handshake was firm, the American voice modulated with assurance.

"Monica has been telling me all about you . . ."

I came back at him in the frivolous mood of the party. "Not *all*, I hope!"

He gave a polite little laugh. "She's been praising you up to the skies."

"Kerry's the very best assistant I've ever had," Monica declared.

"You've never had an assistant before," I pointed out dryly.

"Doesn't that just prove what I've been saying?"

Sam Tracy's eyes shared the joke with me. But the possessive hand on Monica's arm was evidence of his attachment to her. It didn't surprise me. She was such a vital, alive personality that I wondered if any man could be entirely Monica-proof.

I reckoned I'd been mighty lucky myself to meet up with Monica Halliday-Browne. For her, though, the circumstances that had brought us together were less happy, briefly clouding the blue sky of her life. Monica had become a victim of hives, and hated having her flawless skin marred by ugly red weals.

She'd been put on to Dr. Malcolm Stewart just in time. In time I mean,

3

before his own failing health forced him to retire. Dr. Stewart had a canny instinct when it came to difficult allergies, and in no time at all he'd nailed down feathers as the culprit. Being his secretary, I'd got to know Monica pretty well during her course of desensitising injections. The minute she learned that I'd be out of a job when the doctor quit working, she was full of sympathetic concern.

"We'll have to do something about that!" she cried.

I was touched by her interest. Not that I was *worried* about the future — I was reasonably capable, and good jobs in London were plentiful. But right then, with my sister Annabel just married and prancing off to a new and exciting life in Canada, I was feeling a bit fed up. I yearned for something exciting to happen to me, too. The exotic Monica Halliday-Browne held out great promise.

Monica apparently made a habit of doing the unexpected. Her career to date, punctuated by an occasional husband, had included running a marriage bureau in Rio de Janerio and an English woollens boutique on the Costa Brava.

4

The latest scheme, I gathered, was to write a book — a sort of textbook of Continental eating places. But being Monica she didn't intend dealing with anything so mundane as food. Other people, she explained airily, had coped with that aspect. What she planned was to dig out the places with real atmosphere; places where you could expect to dine in intriguing company.

"And you shall come with me as my assistant," she announced.

I was taken aback. "But what should I have to do?"

"Oh . . . er . . . advise me, and . . . " She waved her hands vaguely. "All sorts of things."

I knew perfectly well that she had manufactured her need of an assistant out of pure sweetness of nature. But a trip around Europe with Monica was just the sort of tonic I needed. I lulled my stirring conscience, and accepted the job hastily. Somehow or other I was determined to prove myself really useful to her.

We started three weeks later by coming to Italy.

The idea was to work on a comprehensive

survey of the restaurants of Rome. So what were we doing spending an entire evening at a purely private party? Already I'd given up trying to find the logic behind Monica's sudden impulses. For her, life had to be fun or there was no point in living.

Monica swooped off to greet yet another of her numberless friends with Sam in close tow.

At last I was alone, my attention free. But then, to my dismay, I caught the eye of Guido Zampini, fat and hairy and oilily unattractive. I watched him nod to his companions and start waddling across in my direction. As our host, I suppose I owed him something. But just then I didn't choose to parry his smarmy compliments. I gave him a faint smile and turned quickly away, as if I hadn't recognised his obvious intention.

I swung back to face the spot where the dark-haired Englishman had been standing. Fancy going and disappearing like that, just when I needed him! Standing there eyeing me one minute, and then . . . gone!

I'd forgotten I didn't know him from

Adam; forgotten we'd never so much as said 'hallo'. My eyes began to search the room rather wildly.

"Hallo!" The voice, soft and full of vibrant depth, came from six inches behind my ear.

I bounced round, and it was as much as I could do not to yelp 'Where have you *been*?'

He was grinning down at me, much too cocksure of himself. "Were you looking for someone special?"

I shook my head weakly. Usually, I'm not short of things to say.

He wasted no time at all. "I'm Philip Rainsby. And you?"

"Kerry Lyndon . . . "

"Kerry! I like that. Could it be a bit Irish?"

"Oh, way back. My maternal great-grandfather."

"And you're on holiday . . . ?" he finished.

"Well, not exactly."

"Oh . . . ?"

I was recovering my self-composure. I decided there was no harm explaining how I came to be in Rome, so I told

7

him a bit about Monica.

"Fascinating!" he said. "Getting a living out of having yourself a good time."

"And what brings you to Rome?" I asked. "Business or pleasure?"

He looked straight at me. Was it still mockery that crinkled his eyes?

"At the present moment," he murmured softly, "it is pure, unadulterated pleasure."

"You know what I mean."

He laughed suddenly and wrinkled up his nose. "I'm on a business trip."

"What line are you in?"

I was trying to keep this conversation on a manageable basis. I had a powerful idea that Philip Rainsby was after just the opposite.

He seemed reluctant to tell me about himself. "Well, if you must know, I'm in the highly romantic trade of selling electric switchgear."

"That's nice," I muttered feebly. I couldn't help a feeling of letdown. There was nothing in the world I knew less about, or cared less about for that matter. A man like Philip Rainsby should have been in a far more momentous kind of job.

He took my arm suddenly. "Let's get out of here."

We'd known one another for about five minutes! Literally!

"I'd prefer to stay, thank you," I said, primly and quite untruthfully.

"But it's so hot and crowded. And everybody should see Rome by moonlight. When in Rome, you know . . . "

"I doubt," I replied carefully, "if even the Romans would countenance such exceeding rapidity."

He let go my arm to laugh. "Okay Kerry — we'll play it your way."

But as it turned out, he made most of the rules of the game. I struggled to hang on to the last shreds of my sanity. I'd never believed in love at first sight; I'd never believed in destiny. But tonight everything that had ever happened to me before was unimportant. The fact that I was a moderately intelligent girl, a daughter of the twentieth century, counted for nothing at all. I was living in a fairy story and I had just met my prince.

I doubt if I spoke two words to any other person for the rest of the evening.

When at last Philip delivered me back

to the hotel in a taxi, he arranged to ring me in the morning.

"Good and early," he said. "And we'll fix something exciting to do."

"But not for either lunch or dinner," I reminded him. "Monica will be needing me then."

I doubted it actually. Monica hadn't up till now shown all that much devotion to duty. But I had to play it fair and be around in case she wanted me.

Philip's eyes held mind, staking his claim. I refused to be tempted.

He grinned ruefully. "All right, I won't interfere with your work. As a matter of fact I ought to be doing some myself."

We hung about the hotel lobby, not wanting to part. I was conscious of the night porter's bored interest, but I didn't care.

At last Philip took both my hands in his. "Good night, Kerry darling. Until tomorrow."

Upstairs, I glanced into Monica's room. She wasn't back yet, and I was glad. I didn't want to talk to her just then. I tumbled happily into bed, and slept and dreamt the night away. I came to when Monica burst into my room, and threw back the curtains to reveal broad sunsoaked daylight.

"Eight o'clock, Kerry my pet," she carolled gaily. Nothing could dampen Monica's zest for living. She seemed to possess the physical resources of a bouncing teenager, rather that a woman pulling forty — and on a pretty long rope at that.

She was flitting around in a chiffon *negligé* like some gorgeous orange butterfly.

"Now tell me, Kerry, how did you like my Sam?"

"Very much," I said honestly. I wished I could match her by asking how she liked my Philip.

"Sam's always been after me," she said complacently, perching herself on the edge of my bed. Somehow she managed to loll comfortably and stay straight-backed at one and the same time. "I met him just before I married Michael, you know."

"Michael?"

"Yes pet, my third husband. The wedding was all fixed, you see, so there was nothing I could do about it at the time. I always preferred Sam, though."

It was no good trying to apply ordinary standards to Monica Halliday-Browne. She was a law unto herself. By now I'd learned to give up being astonished. I just took her as she came.

"So what happened?" I asked cautiously.

Monica reached across and picked up my bedside phone, asking for room service. "*Caffe e latte, caro mio,*" she trilled. She replaced the receiver delicately, and regarded me with a wicked glint in her blue-green eyes.

"The Michael episode," she remarked with firm dismissal, "is over and done with. Sam is back in my life now — and for good."

That did take me by surprise. "For good?"

Monica had the grace to colour slightly. But through the flush her eyes shone with delight.

"Sam has asked me to marry him, and I've accepted."

"Oh Monica, how lovely!" I was genuinely pleased for her, because she was so obviously pleased for herself. And I had liked Sam.

"I'm flying to the United States with him tomorrow."

My background didn't allow for such frivolity. Dad had been a small town doctor, and my mother had run our home with calm, unruffled order. I still couldn't adjust to the idea of dropping all your plans at a moment's notice. I couldn't easily keep pace with this off-with-the-old-and-on-with-the-new malarky.

All I could manage was a weak repetition of Monica's words. "Flying to the States tomorrow?"

"Yes, Kerry, and we'll be married by evening. I must get my outfit over here, before we leave."

I floundered around a bit. "But Monica, have you really thought what you're doing ... ?"

"My pet, I've thought of little else for simply *hours.*" She regarded me seriously. "Marriage is a big step in a woman's life — I ought to know that."

Only then did it hit me that I too was going to be affected by Monica's impetuous decision. Why did it have to happen now, just when Rome had become the most desirable city in the whole

13

world? Why did this exciting new life have to fold up on me without warning?

I suppose my gloomy face gave me away.

"What is it, Kerry?" Monica asked anxiously. "What's the matter?"

"Nothing," I said quickly. But I couldn't entirely keep the self-pitying misery out of my voice.

Monica jumped up and bent over the bed to put her arms round me. "Darling, how could I have been so beastly? Full of myself, my own happiness, and not a thought for you!"

"It's all right," I muttered.

"But it's not all right! I persuade you to come out here, and then just up and quit."

"But . . . "

She wasn't listening. Pacing away from me now, over to the window and then back, Monica was lost in thought. Once again she was feverishly making plans for me. "Of course, pet, you won't have to worry about the financial aspect. Would three months — no, *six* months in lieu of notice be okay? And your plane ticket back to London."

14

It was incredibly generous of her, and I couldn't possibly accept so much. "But it's not that," I said sadly. "I don't want to go back to London."

"Well then, you shan't." I swear that right then Monica was thinking more about my predicament than her own wedding.

The waiter came in with the coffee. Monica tossed him a brilliant though abstracted smile, and he departed well pleased with himself.

Suddenly Monica stopped prowling and snapped her fingers in the air. "I've got it! Adeline Harcourt."

"Who's she?" I asked. Very dimly the name echoed in my mind, but I couldn't pin it down.

Monica regarded me with pity. "Not to have seen Adeline Harcourt as Lady Macbeth is not to have lived."

"Oh, she's an actress?"

"She *was*, my pet. One of the truly greats. But of course she was rather before your time. Dear Adeline must be well into her seventies by now." Monica picked up the phone again, jigging it impatiently. "Get me Miss Adeline Harcourt," she said in English. "She's staying at the Prima Astoria — I think."

I lay back and waited, reckoning I'd learn quicker that way than trying to probe the mystery of Monica's mind.

It never seemed to take her long to get put through on the phone. In a few seconds she was chirping. "Adeline . . . oh darling, did I wake you?"

The receiver quacked, and Monica held it a distasteful three inches from her ear. "Well, never mind — the damage is done now, isn't it? Listen darling, I've got just the person to help you run that great guest house of yours."

The quacking was quieter now, and I could almost imagine a puzzled note to it.

Monica plunged in again. "But *of course* you need an assistant, Adeline. Why should you *slave* away all the while, now you've reached a time of life when you should be taking it easy . . . No, I did *not* mean you're *ancient*, darling. But let's face it, with all your money, why *should* you . . . ?"

I was fearfully embarrassed. Obviously, Monica was selling me hard to this

16

unknown woman. She herself had made a job for me, and she refused to see why someone else shouldn't do the same.

I shook my head at her, frowning and gesticulating fiercely. Monica chose not to notice, casually turning her back on me.

"But darling, Kerry is absolutely ... She's been my assistant for simply ... *of course* I'd like to keep her myself, only how can I ... ?"

There was a pause; then Monica continued in a little rush. "Oh, didn't I explain, darling? I'm going to marry Sam Tracy. Yes, after all this time ... "

It went on for some minutes. Feeling helpless, I poured the coffee and had time to drink it before she'd finished talking.

Monica put down the phone in triumph. "You're to go and see Adeline before lunch — one o'clock, she said."

"But how can I? There isn't any job, is there? She doesn't want me."

Monica merely smiled smugly. "Oh, I think she will. You just go along and talk it over with her, my pet. You can't refuse me that."

I wasn't in a mood to argue any more. I badly wanted to remain in Italy, and

17

after all, Adeline Harcourt *had* agreed to see me.

Monica swallowed half a cup of coffee, and floated out of my room. I looked at my watch. Eight-forty.

What, I wondered, had Philip meant by good and early? Would he ring about nine?

I decided to be ready and waiting for his call, so I jumped out of bed and bathed and dressed in a hurry. But not too quickly — I put some concentrated care into the final polish . . .

I stuck to my room, close beside the phone. By nine-thirty the heat of the day was coming up, and some of my polish was losing its sparkle.

By ten-thirty I was feeling pretty limp. I abandoned the phone long enough to go to the bathroom for another wash, and then re-applied my make-up.

By eleven I'd almost given up. Fighting off despair, I went over and shut the windows. Why had I thought Rome a gaily bustling city? It was just plain noisy!

By eleven-thirty I *had* given up, finally and for ever. Damn the man! Damn all men! It would be a mighty long time before I made such an utter fool of myself again. But just in case something unavoidable had delayed him, I still hung about in my room.

I'd lost all heart for the appointment with Adeline Harcourt now. Why stay in Rome and be reminded? But out of courtesy I had to go through the motions, so I changed into something more suitable for a job applicant — a cool-looking pale green and white Courtelle outfit. Soon after twelve-thirty I emerged for the first time that day.

It was only a short way to the Prima Astoria. I decided to walk, strolling easily in the hot sun. I had to admit, reluctantly, that despite everything Rome was a lovely place. And after all, it didn't belong to Philip Rainsby. With the logic of my Irish great-grandfather, I decided that if I ever ran into the man again in Rome, I wouldn't give him the satisfaction of knowing I'd run away on his account.

On my left the raised terrace of a classy hotel was brightly decked in coloured awning and sun umbrellas. The tables were crowded with pre-lunch drinkers,

19

but a man and woman sitting close to the balustrade became the instant focus of my attention.

My eyes riveted on them.

Philip Rainsby, laughing and joking with a woman! A brash over-ripe blondie type of maybe thirty-five plus.

From the way he sharply bent his head as I went past, it looked like he'd seen me, too. But he gave not the smallest blink of recognition.

I lifted my chin, and strode on briskly.

2

I WALKED so fast and furiously that I arrived at the Prima Astoria in a sweat. Fortunately I had five minutes in hand, so I skulked behind a bank of potted pink hydrangeas in the cool lounge, and slowly simmered down.

At five to one precisely I went across to the reception desk and asked for Miss Harcourt. I still hadn't reached a decision about whether or not I wanted a job with her, even if she was prepared to have me. I'd not been thinking about that.

Obediently, I tailed the bellboy across expanses of opulent floor, let myself be wafted upwards in a silent lift, and tottered after him through a long corridor.

When he tapped on a door and held it open for me, I went in like an automaton. I was too bemused to get more than the vaguest impression of the apartment, except that it was rather ornately furnished.

At first I thought I was alone, until a

jewelled hand, followed by a slender arm, lifted itself gracefully above the back of a sofa set facing one of the tall windows. The index finger raised aloft, beckoned. At the same moment a voice, a thrillingly resonant contralto-deep voice, broke the silence.

"Of course she won't, *caro mio.* There is no earthly reason why she should ever discover . . . "

Miss Adeline Harcourt, I gathered, was speaking on the telephone.

The bellboy closed the door behind me. Obeying the imperious instructions of the still-raised arm, I went across the huge room. Miss Harcourt, stretched comfortably on the sofa, smiled a little absently and motioned me to sit down on a nearby chair.

"But you worry yourself too much," she went on. He voice fascinated me. Not particularly loud, it filled every corner of the room; I could well imagine how it used to fill every corner of a great auditorium. " . . . listen . . . " she was saying, "just a little help with the domestic side, that is all. I tell you, it is of no consequence to us . . . "

I sat and observed Miss Harcourt discreetly. Monica had told me she was well into her seventies. From her appearance, though, it would have seemed ungenerous to label her even as much as sixty. Her easily lounging figure was supple; the gesticulating arms had the lazy grace of youth.

A formidable old lady, I thought! I began to wonder if, after all, I might not enjoy working for her. Monica had been fun. Adeline Harcourt promised to be stimulating too, in a different way.

She put down the phone at last, and switched her full attention upon me. Her smile was no longer preoccupied; it belonged to me — warm, friendly, and quite utterly candid.

"Forgive me . . . "

"Not at all, Miss Harcourt."

"You look charming, my dear. So pretty!"

My deflated ego swelled with the puff. This woman had obviously been a real beauty in her time — the fine bone structure of her face was evidence of that.

"So you are coming to help me at the

Villa Stella d'Oro?"

"Well — I'm not sure ... "

"Not sure? But I thought it was all fixed. Monica told me on the telephone that you were anxious to find another post here in Italy."

Quite suddenly I'd come to a definite decision. "Yes, I do, Miss Harcourt. But I wasn't sure if you'd really want me."

"Is there any reason why I should not?"

"It's just that I got the idea you weren't really needing any help," I explained, a bit uncomfortably. "It sounded as if Monica was rather pressuring you into it."

"Nobody pressures me into anything." A shadow crossed her face, as though she was trying to convince herself as well as me. But I could easily have imagined it, because her mobile features were relaxed again into a pleasant smile. "I confess I did have certain ... reservations at first. But now I have decided that Monica's suggestion is an excellent one. The villa is too much for me to manage on my own. It will suit me very nicely to have you there to help."

24

"You realise I've had no experience of this sort of thing?"

She snorted delicately. "You are intelligent, are you not?"

"I hope so."

"Intelligence is all that is required in any business undertaking."

She picked up the phone again, and spoke briskly. "I have a reservation on the Catania plane this afternoon. Book an additional seat, if you please."

I felt hopelessly confused. Surely the extra reservation must be intended for me? For the moment I couldn't place Catania, but clearly it must be at some distance if we were to fly there. And all the time I'd been taking it for granted that Adeline Harcourt's guest house was not far from Rome.

Miss Harcourt had replaced the phone. "Salary we will discuss later. You will find me not ungenerous. Now, will you be here with your luggage by three o'clock at the very latest?"

Feeling I was probably putting my foot slap in the middle of something silly, I asked: "Where are we going, Miss Harcourt?"

"Where?" Her sharp look doubted my sanity. "To the *Villa Stella d'Oro*, of course. Where else?"

"Monica didn't happen to mention where you villa was. I rather thought if must be near Rome."

"Oh, I see." She smiled, relieved, I think, to discover that I was not an imbecile. "No, it is a long way from Rome. The *Stella d'Oro* has a magnificent situation in the hill behind Taormina. We get quite remarkable view of Etna."

Etna! But Mount Etna was in Sicily! So, now I came to think of it, was Catania.

How could I possibly go flying off to Sicily just like that? It must be hundreds of miles from Rome — way down south. An island in the Mediterranean.

I considered the alternatives. I might try to find another job in Rome. But what sort of job could I hope to get? An English girl whose Italian was decidedly ropey — one might almost say non-existent. A girl whose idea of local geography was so vague she hadn't been able to pin down Catania.

Rome, I reckoned, was out as far as a

job was concerned.

What else, then? Go back to London, tail between my legs? Admit defeat? Admit the exotic life was not for me?

Going to Sicily wouldn't be admitting defeat. It wouldn't be a matter of running away from Philip Rainsby. I'd been offered a job there, a job that grew more attractive every moment I thought about it.

An island in the Mediterranean! A villa in the sun!

"I think I'm going to like Sicily," I said impulsively.

Adeline Harcourt scooped up my agreement with a quick smile. "You will love poor Sicily," she pronounced in that richly vibrant voice. "One cannot help loving her. She has seen so much tragedy, yet for all that she is beautiful. Beautiful!"

It was like a curtain speech. A curtain coming down on my past existence. Soon, a new act would begin.

I had thought it impossible to switch the direction of life within the space of a couple of hours. But in practice I found it not only possible, but highly stimulating.

Naturally, Monica rallied round, delighted that her plan for me had worked out. Having spent the entire morning trousseau shopping, she came back tired. But she readily skipped lunch to dash round a large department store with me, hastily sorting out the things she insisted I should need in Sicily. And afterwards she found time to come to the airport to see us off.

Next morning she would be leaving Rome herself, going direct to New York with her Sam.

When we were airborne, settling back comfortably with a long cool drink of vermouth and soda, Adeline Harcourt began to tell me about the villa with the romantic name. *Stella d'Oro* — Star of Gold.

"It was given me by my beloved Vittorio," she said with a happy sigh. "Such a generous man, Vittorio. He could never do enough for me."

When I remarked innocently that he sounded the perfect husband, she burst into a peal of merry laughter. In her penetrating voice she announced to a fascinated planeload of passengers that

Vittorio d'Azeglio had been her lover, not her husband.

"It made little difference, though. We were faithful for oh — so long. Then poor Vittorio died. His arteries . . . "

"I'm sorry," I muttered, embarrassed.

"Don't be, my dear. If your own life holds as much happiness as mine has done, you will be very content."

She sighed again, enjoying her memories.

"I gave up the stage when I lost my Vittorio, and came to live in Sicily permanently. My heart was there, you see. Besides, I was never cut out for *elderly* parts." She spoke the word like it was sour on the tongue.

I tried to get an idea of the job I was expected to do.

"Oh, just to give me a hand in running the villa. You will have to learn my little peculiarities and act accordingly."

"How many guests do you have?" I asked.

"Never many at one time. You see, I run the *Stella d'Oro* for pleasure rather than for money. It would seem such an empty house with just myself. I like to have people around me." She added quickly, "But I am very choosy. I only take those who have been personally recommended."

I got the feeling she wasn't terribly keen to discuss the management of her guest house. Maybe it was altogether too workaday a subject. Instead, I asked her to tell me about Sicily, and that touched the button. We were in fact so preoccupied, Adeline holding forth and I an eager listener, that we almost missed the approach from the air. I was just in time to pick out the great bulk of Mount Etna before we landed at Catania.

The drive to the *Villa Stella d'Oro* was about forty miles, I gathered. Miss Harcourt had phoned ahead from Rome, instructing one of her staff to meet us with the car. But it had not turned up. She was just beginning to tut impatiently when a cheerful voice hit us from behind.

"Hi there, Adeline!"

We both wheeled round. Grinning down at us was an incredibly good-looking man. He was casually dressed in a blue striped sweat shirt and white cotton slacks. His lean face was tanned whole shades deeper than mere bronze.

"Giles darling!" Adeline cried. "How delightful. But why are *you* here?"

"For the pleasure of driving you home," he said gallantly. "What else?" But he was taking a good slow look at me as he spoke.

Adeline Harcourt hadn't missed a thing. "This is Kerry Lyndon, and she has come here to do a job." She winked at me. "I stress this fact, my dear, to disabuse Giles right from the outset."

"Nobody," he said, shaking his head solemnly, "but *nobody* comes to Sicily to work."

"Now Giles, be quiet," said Adeline. "Kerry, this is Giles Yorke. A dear friend of mine and a clever artist when he chooses to exert himself. But he is also rather a naughty boy."

Giles led the way over to his car, a snazzy red sports job, wide open to the evening sun. He signalled the hovering porter to pile our luggage in the back.

"In with you, girls." Giles opened the passenger door for us. But as Adeline started to climb in, he put a hand on her arms. "Let Kerry get squashed in

31

the middle. You'll be more comfortable on the outside."

"I shall be more comfortable, young man," said Adeline severely, "sitting next to you. This way I can be confident you will pay some attention to your driving."

We left the airport just like we were taking off, and were soon on a coastal road. The scenery was fantastic, but with the flow of chat I didn't get a chance to look around much. To our right was vivid blue sea; to our left, the foothills of Etna. At breakneck speed we flashed through a landscape of black rock, verdant lemon groves, and a mesmerising carpet of brilliant flowers.

"And what," yelled Giles Yorke, "is Kerry in the scheme of things?"

"She is going to help me run the *Stella d'Oro.* To relieve me of some of the burden."

"But I mean, what about . . . ?"

Adeline cut in with snappy decision. "I don't know what you mean, Giles. I've just told you, Kerry has come to help me. And that's all there is to it."

I glanced past her profile and caught

Gile's puzzled frown. Then Adeline shifted in her seat, and cut off my view.

There was a tangible spikiness in the atmosphere. I couldn't imagine what it was all about, but I was uncomfortably aware that in some way it concerned me.

In an effort to take the strain off, I asked Giles about his painting.

"What sort of things do you do?"

"Oh, this and that," he said carelessly. "Mostly pot-boiling views of the bay to flog to tourists. I have to keep that old wolf from knocking at my door."

Adeline had entirely recovered her good spirits. "As I explained to you, Kerry, he is a fine artist. But Giles is far too frivolous, so be on your guard."

The road jerked us upward, flicking to the left and right, circling a giant's tooth of hard rock that sprouted a curious spiny succulent bush from every smallest crevice. We passed very little other traffic. At one point a flock of hens were sleepily scratching dust in the middle of the road. They scurried from under our wheels with resentful squawks. As we accelerated away again, a snatched glimpse through a gateway showed me a large rambling house. A group of children were sitting in a circle on the grass, singing.

"What's that? A school?"

"It is the convent of *Santa Teresa*," Adeline told me. "For orphans. The sisters are wonderful, but there are so many children and not enough money. I do what little I can to help them."

We hadn't much further to go. Zooming around a last bend, a blaze of yellow flowers on the bank, we shot through black wrought-iron gates, open to the road. Without pause we raced on, scrunching the immaculate drive of a formal Italian garden.

I saw neat, low-trimmed hedges, exuberant marble statuary, and the dark straight fingers of cypresses. And then we had stopped by some wide, shallow steps. The white walls of the *Villa Stella d'Oro* glowed golden in the setting sun. Canopied balconies and wide, graceful arches made an immediate impression of cool spaciousness.

The silence following the cutting of the motor was broken by excited twitterings. The staff were gathered in true old-time style to greet the return of their mistress. A fat, sweating, prematurely-aged woman and a ravishing black-haired girl of seventeen or so were both delighting in the moment, laughing and crying and wringing their hands in abandoned ecstasy. But the third member of the group did not outwardly share their joy. He was a tall young man; slim, swarthy, with the smug arrogance of a male who knows he is good to look at. Darkly sullen, his eyes were fixed upon me.

Adeline, swinging smoothly out of the car, greeted the women affectionately. The man she acknowledged with caution, and what looked like doubt at the back of her eyes.

She introduced me. They had known of my coming, of course, through her phone call from Rome. I was prepared for a certain degree of unwelcome; I was a stranger, a foreigner, whose job it would be to tell them what to do.

But Maria the fat cook, and Luciana the pretty young housemaid, showed no sign of resentment; only warmingly cheerful smiles.

The man Carlo was quite another

matter. I learned that he was Maria's nephew, waiter and general handyman at the *Stella d'Oro.* He stared at me boldly, sneered, half-turned his back and muttered rudely under his breath. It was a virtuoso display of insolence yet all done with such subtlety that I am sure nobody else even noticed.

If this was a foretaste of what was to come, I could count on trouble with Carlo. Still, I wouldn't anticipate; I'd settle in and take things as I found them.

Adeline Harcourt was maddeningly imprecise about my duties. She seemed to treat me more as a guest than as an employee, and I found myself quite unable to pin her down to anything positive.

"Time enough to find you more to do when you are properly settled in," she said cheerfully, when I pressed her again on the day after my arrival.

"*More* to do!" I protested. "So far I've had next to nothing."

But she merely smiled serenely. "Forget your precipitate northern temperament, Kerry darling," she said, promoting me in her endearment scale. "You must adjust to the Sicilian pace now. Down here we take life much more easily."

They certainly did! Three servants, Adeline and me, all deployed for the benefit of just two guests, a pair of young honeymooners from Austria. It was a crazy situation.

Adeline, no doubt unwittingly, made things more difficult for me by encouraging Giles to stick around the villa. And he on his part seemed glad of any excuse to desert his studio.

The trouble was, I liked Giles. In fact, I liked him a lot. He was gay and amusing. He certainly had a carefree attitude to life, but then I'd never believed there was any particular virtue in taking a solemn view. Giles lived the way he wanted, and did nobody any harm that I could see.

His keen interest in me was enormously flattering. If I'd not been scared of getting caught on the rebound after that deathblow from Philip, I might have let Giles know how much I liked him. But as it was, I stayed markedly cool.

I managed to hold him off all the first day. But after lunch on the second, when the staff were off duty and Adeline was taking a siesta upstairs, Giles caught me by the door of the kitchen.

"You keep pacing around like a caged animal, Kerry."

I pretended not to notice that his face was barely six inches from mine. "Go away. I've got work to do . . . "

"And all the time in the world to do it in." He jerked his head in a quick grin. "Relax, Kerry. You're in Sicily now."

"But I'm supposed to be here to do a job."

"Stop arguing with your good luck." He leaned forward suddenly so that his lips were against mine. I felt my resistance dissolving. Was there some magic in the Sicilian air that made me want to let him kiss me?

Whatever it was, I struggled against the impulse, pushing myself back to the wall. But I couldn't escape him. His arms were tight around me, drawing me towards him again. I could feel the supple warmth of his lean body. His teeth shone white against deep-bronze skin.

"No Giles, don't," I said sharply. "Somebody might come."

He laughed. "Wouldn't that be just too awful — for someone to catch sight of a pair of lovers kissing, here in Sicily . . . "

"Don't be ridiculous," I said, struggling out of his arms.

He let me go, just retaining one hand firmly in his own.

"You can't stop me hoping," he said lightly.

I couldn't find it in me to brush Giles off more decisively. Maybe my damaged pride needed the tonic of having a man interested in me.

Together we strolled out to the shady loggia, a green haven of trailing creepers and vines. It was cool and refreshing. Beyond, the heat of afternoon sun shimmered above parching grass.

Giles was very much at home at the *Stella d'Oro*. He wandered back indoors, and emerged a moment later carrying a tray. Just iced water and lemon juice; without any sugar at all it was marvellously tangy.

A little fountain tinkled as a background. We lounged in long cane chairs, sipping the drinks, talking in a desultory way. Giles asked what had brought me to

Sicily, and I explained a bit about myself and my job with Monica.

I didn't say a word about Philip Rainsby.

Giles gave me a slow, appraising survey of a look. "I thought maybe it was a man that brought you belting over here."

"Of course it's not a man!" There was acid in my voice.

"I meant," he remarked mildly, "a man you are running away from. An unhappy memory, maybe?"

"You're crazy. I needed a job, that's all."

"Only, there isn't much work for you to do?" His eyes narrowed. "It almost makes me wonder if you haven't got some sort of hold on Adeline."

"What are you talking about now?"

He shrugged. "Maybe you know something the old girl doesn't want made public."

Swift anger rose in me. "Are you suggesting that I'm blackmailing Miss Harcourt?"

I began to get up, but from such a low, reclining position it wasn't an easy thing to do with dignity. Giles put out a lazy hand and held me back.

"Calm down, Kerry. I was only kidding."

"Well, I don't think it was funny, that's all."

But I stayed. Giles sipped his drink for a minute. Then, with mock contrition, he raised his eyes to mine. "Am I forgiven?"

I had to grin at him. "I must admit I feel a bit of a fraud, though. We could easily have a lot more people staying here. A fabulous place like this, and bang in the middle of the season ... "

"There are some new people coming tomorrow," he said.

"Oh, really?"

"Yes. A couple from England, I hear. And another chap on his own."

I felt piqued that Giles should know more than I did about expected guests. He must have seen my annoyance, because he added hastily: "Adeline just happened to mention it."

"Well, it's a pity she didn't happen to mention it to me!" But I felt hurt more than angry. And after all, Giles wasn't the one to blame. "Oh, never mind ... " I stretched back luxuriously in my chair.

"It's too gloriously hot to quarrel about anything."

He gave me an amused glance, nodding with approval.

"Now you're getting the idea of Sicily," he said. "The main thing is to relax and stop worrying about things that don't really matter anyway. Enjoy yourself."

"I can see it could be a pleasant life," I admitted.

"Take it from one who knows! And as a first lesson in the art of living, you shall come on a little excursion with me tomorrow."

3

AFTERNOON tea was the social high spot of the day at the *Villa Stella d'Oro.* Adeline made quite a ceremony of it. She presided over the wagon, wielding an exquisite silver teapot and water jug. It gave her an unmatched opportunity to dazzle everyone with her dramatic talents, and I guessed this was the only reason for sticking to so English a habit. All other meals at the villa were strictly Italian-style.

But that afternoon we were a small party, only Giles and I were joining her for tea. The honeymooners were out, apparently forgetting the time. We sat in the salon, long windows thrown wide to the loggia.

"I hear from Giles we are expecting three more guests tomorrow," I said, deliberately revealing a mild resentment.

But Adeline didn't seem to notice. "I only hope we shall like them. It is so trying if people are not *simpatico.*"

Then she added casually: "By the way, Signor Zampini is also coming for a few days. You met him in Rome, I believe?"

"Yes. Monica took me along to a party at his place." I remembered the man particularly because he'd struck me as so repulsive. "I didn't realise that you knew him, Miss Harcourt."

Delicately, Adeline added cream to a cup of tea. "Oh yes indeed, we are old, old friends."

The thought of having Signor Zampini so close at hand gave me no pleasure. I was surprised, too. I wondered what on earth Adeline Harcourt, one-time queen of the London stage, could possibly have in common with this fat and hairy Italian.

It struck me as odd that, since they were such old friends, she hadn't been at his party in Rome. I knew for a fact she'd been in the city that evening.

Giles drifted into the conversation, talking about the proposed jaunt as though it were already fixed, taking it quite for granted that I could go. I felt horribly uncomfortable at his easy assumption that my job could be treated so lightly.

But I needn't have worried. Adeline was enthusiastic. "It's a very good idea for you to get to know your way around the island. How else can you appear knowledgeable when guests ask for information?"

"But oughtn't I to be here when the new people arrive?"

Adeline blithely dismissed this as quite unnecessary. In fact, I rather got the impression she would prefer me to be out.

Summer had come early, even for Sicily. The heat was mounting, each day up on the one before. When we set out the sun was already high, bouncing up from the ground almost as fiercely as it glared down from the sky.

Giles planned to drive me up Etna. "Not all the way, though. After six or seven thousand feet the road fizzles out. Of course, you can always walk the rest, if you like."

I glanced at him suspiciously, wondering if he was pulling my leg.

Actually, I found Giles surprisingly well-informed. He spoke with compassion of the dreadful earthquakes Sicily had suffered, the Messina disaster early in the century, and the recent upheavals on the western side of the island. He told me about some of Etna's worst eruptions, way back. "Still, maybe the old girl isn't all bad, considering this lot comes from the filthy muck she throws up from her innards."

'This lot' was the lower slopes, lush vineyards and terraced orchards of lemon and orange. Olives too, and everything imaginable crammed in. Not the tiniest fragment of soil was allowed to go to waste.

Quite suddenly Giles swerved off the road. He pulled up beside the entrance to a café. I glimpsed a sprawling white building half hidden by trees, with tables and chairs dotted around a paved courtyard.

"We'll have a drink here, and push on nearer the crater for lunch," he said. "Then we'll have time for a slow amble back to the villa for tea."

"This trip sounds more gastronomic than educational," I laughed.

Giles didn't laugh. "I don't intend it to be either."

It was the sort of remark, I decided, best left well alone.

Maybe I was slowing down to a Sicilian pace after all. It was so easy just to sit back and let things happen. The idea of a long cool drink in that shade-dappled garden was heaven. Even the feather-soft air seemed to be asking what was the hurry. Wouldn't Etna still be there tomorrow?

In the café garden we made for a small arbour that had a view right up to Etna's summit. But half way across, Giles switched direction.

"It'll be cooler inside," he muttered.

I protested. "But it's gorgeous out here. And I wanted to enjoy the view."

"You'll be sick of that view soon enough," he said rather sourly. He reached for my hand, and firmly marched towards the glass door leading inside.

I threw a wistful glance over my shoulder, and caught a swift impression of a familiar face. Still towed by Giles, I took a second look back.

Signor Zampini — the fat and greasy Guido Zampini! He looked as repellent as ever, uncomfortably hot in a dark blue suit tight-buttoned across his massive paunch.

Giles skipped up a couple of shallow steps. I fell up them, nearly capsizing. As I swung round to save myself, my last flash took in Zampini's companions, a man and a woman. The man I didn't know. The woman I did — oh my God I did!

I'd seen her just once before. Back in Rome, sitting on a hotel terrace, big-eyeing Philip Rainsby.

"Giles!" I yelled. "Wait a minute."

He almost dragged me the last yard. We were inside the café, door shut behind us, before he stopped and faced me.

"What's up, Kerry?"

I was on the edge of telling him, but I held back. It was something too personal to talk about. And I had an odd feeling there were wider implications I couldn't yet analyse.

"What's the matter?" Giles repeated, looking a bit anxious.

I improvised. "You nearly had me over then, that's what."

He grinned. "Sorry. I wanted to grab us a nice table."

I couldn't see what he was flapping about. Most people seemed to share my own preference for the tables in the garden. The restaurant itself was almost empty.

Giles must have had another reason for his abrupt change of mind. It was as though he too had spotted somebody outside, somebody he wanted to avoid.

The fat Italian was a likely candidate. Giles must surely know Guido Zampini, I reckoned. Perhaps he disliked Adeline's old friend as much as I did.

I was cheated of my cool drink too. We gulped down a hurried Martini in the uncomfortable overwarm restaurant. And then we were on our way again, attacking the mountain road like hell was on our tail.

My memory of that mad drive up Etna is hazy. Vaguely, I recall a falling-off of cultivation as we climbed higher. Then there were trees, I think, before a curiously forbidding region of black desert. I was certainly glad of the coat Giles had persuaded me to bring. In the heat down below, it had seemed impossible that I should need it. But high up the air was chilly and the wind biting.

We lunched at a sort of clubhouse at the end of the road. Giles ate ravenously, saying the cold air gave him an appetite. But I wasn't hungry. I couldn't get out of my mind a picture of three people at a table in a café garden thousands of feet below us. They'd be gone by now, but in my mind they were still there, talking earnestly.

Seeing Zampini was just an unpleasant coincidence. But the sight of that woman had shaken me badly. It reminded me too sharply, too cruelly, of someone I'd thought I was beginning to forget.

Giles made sure we got back to the *Stella d'Oro* in time for the teatime ritual. "It means so much to Adeline," he said lightly. "We mustn't disappoint the old darling by being late."

We had ten minutes to spare before five o'clock deadline. I went straight up to my bedroom to wash off Etna's dust, and slipped into a crisp pink linen dress. I got down to the salon bang on time.

Unexpectedly, it was quite full. Giles was there, of course, lounging easily in an armchair next to Adeline. On her other side were two men I'd not seen before — one rather short, trim and military-looking, with a small neat toothbrush moustache. The other, much younger, was tall and fair, with a paler complexion that looked as if it were new to Sicily.

There were also three people sitting with their backs to me. It was only as they swung round, the men jumping politely to their feet, that I recognised them.

I'd been expecting Guido Zampini to show up at the villa sometime today, so his presence didn't surprise me. Maybe the sight of the other two didn't surprise me all that much either. Maybe I'd feared this ever since seeing the three of them together at the café.

I believe I managed to conjure up a smile. But if so, then it was quite utterly false.

4

ADELINE HARCOURT, queening it over the tea wagon, had all the smooth style of a Mayfair hostess. "Kerry, darling! Do come and meet my friends."

Taking a good strong hold on myself, I went forward.

Adeline began the introductions. "Signor Zampini you have met before. I have known him for oh, so many years ... " She pursed her lips and gave a teasing little shake of her head, as if begging him not to divulge precisely how many years it was. She moved on. "Mr. and Mrs. Blunt, who have come to stay with us for a while ... "

"How do you do?" I murmured.

The man held out a huge hand, thick fingers splayed. "How do, me dear. And none of this Mr. and Mrs. business, if you please. The names are George and Rosie ... "

"Rosalind!" his wife corrected sharply.

Now that I looked at her more closely, I had to admit she was attractive. She had a perfect heart-shaped face, and silky golden-blonde hair that swung to her shoulders. Vivid wide blue eyes gave her a look of fetching innocence. Yet underneath I detected a vein of toughness that maybe only another woman could recognise.

Her husband's grin was entirely fond as he said: "I always call her Rosie. Happen she's as sweet as any rose I ever saw . . ."

"Oh, don't be a damn fool George," she slung back spitefully.

Her voice was strident, and I couldn't place the accent because it was larded over with pretensions to class. The man, however, spoke pure Yorkshire — a no-nonsense, un-polished Yorkshire.

Adeline was continuing with the introductions. The two men beside her, I gathered, were connected with the local police.

" . . . Inspector Vigorelli and his assistant, Cesare Pastore." She became stagily arch. "They pretend they have come for the pleasure of taking tea with me, but I suspect they know all about my wicked criminal activities, and will whisk me away to one of their dungeons at any moment."

I managed to join in the dutiful titter, but the image of a hotel terrace in Rome was dominating my mind. Philip Rainsby and that woman — and I wasn't a bit surprised to discover she was married. I could picture the scene too clearly to doubt their intimacy. There had been a closeness between them that spoke of a whole lot more than casual friendship.

The older police officer had taken my hand and bowed low, clicking his heels smartly. The younger one shook hands, and looked into my eyes.

I became aware I was keeping the men on their feet. I sat down hastily.

Signor Zampini flashed me a gold-dazzling smile, and explained to the others: "Signorina Lyndon was so kind as to come to a little reception I gave in Rome." In spite of his thick charm, I got the impression that for some reason he disliked me, or distrusted me. I remembered how I'd dodged him at the party. Maybe he had recognised that as a deliberate brush-off. I smiled back at him, trying to look amiable. For Miss Harcourt's sake I mustn't offend him any further.

I turned to the woman. "You and your husband have just arrived from Rome?" I wasn't really sure what I hoped to gain by asking about Rome. She was hardly likely to mention Philip.

To my surprise she looked embarrassed and glanced at her husband. Flushing, he flickered his eyes towards Zampini. Following the quick sequence, I was certain that the fat Italian gave a slight nod of assent.

It had all happened so rapidly that the woman's reply could have sounded spontaneous. "Yes, that's right. We flew over from Rome this afternoon."

"This afternoon?" But it was in the morning that I had seen them with Zampini.

"Aye, lass," George Blunt confirmed quickly. "Straight from Rome we've come, and driven up here from Catania."

Just what was going on between these three?

"I don't remember meeting you at the

party," I said, tossing out the bait to both husband and wife.

Rosalind Blunt looked cautiously puzzled, but her husband charged straight in.

"What party would that have been, lass?"

Suddenly I was aware that the rest of the company had become an absorbed audience.

"I mean Signor Zampini's party — the one he mentioned just now."

Both the Blunts started talking at once in their eagerness to deny all previous knowledge of the Italian. "We haven't had the pleasure of meeting Signor Zampini before . . . " she fluttered, while he came in heavily: "Never clapped eyes on the gent until ten minutes ago."

A shiver ran through me, a whisper of . . . not quite fear, but of something pretty unpleasant all the same. Why were the Blunts and Zampini pretending to be strangers?

Come to think of it, there had been a scheming air about the close way they'd talked together at the restaurant table. And I had an uneasy feeling there must be some link with Giles' strange behaviour when he'd abruptly hauled me off indoors. Had he some reason for not wanting me to see these three together?

I glanced at Giles, but he seemed deep in talk with Adeline. He must have heard the Blunt's remark about not knowing Zampini, yet he'd expressed no surprise. Of course, I couldn't be positive he'd spotted that trio in the café garden. Maybe his sudden decision to find a table inside had been for some other reason.

I didn't know what to make of this peculiar set-up, but I was going to have a word with Miss Harcourt about it at the first opportunity. I had to warn her that something underhand was going on. For the moment, though, I'd better play it along, concealing what I knew.

Inspector Vigorelli addressed me with stiff courtesy. "You are coming to live here in *Sicilia*, signorina?"

"For the time being. As long as Miss Harcourt has a use for me."

"Ah yes ... ?" I felt his interest quicken.

Adeline cut in: "Kerry thinks I give her too little to do. But of course coming straight from England she is

57

so headstrong." The firm voice became suddenly tremulous. "It is such a help to have her here — an old woman like me . . . "

On cue, the police inspector jumped in with a gallantry about Adeline's youthful appearance, scorning the very idea of encroaching old age. But having launched herself into the frail old lady act, Adeline wasn't going to abandon it so soon. Now she became a figure of tragedy.

"The sisters of *Santa Teresa* shall have the *Stella d'Oro* when I am gone." She paused, her timing perfect. "And sometimes I think they will not have long to wait."

And then all at once she'd had enough of that. Shooting out a hand towards Giles, she asked if he'd like another cup of tea in a voice that had left tragedy far behind.

George Blunt turned to the inspector, making conversation. "Do you have a lot of crime to deal with here? This er . . . what's its name . . . this *Mafia*? Does it give you much trouble?"

Shock froze the room. Seconds ticked away in silence, while George Blunt stared around bewildered, aware of a blunder without understanding it.

Adeline came to his rescue. "In Sicily," she explained carefully, "one does not speak of the . . . Old Movement. It is considered unlucky."

"I'm very sorry, I'm sure," he said, his bluff face reddening fiercely.

The sticky moment was quickly plastered over with small talk. But I didn't listen, too intent on trying to analyse why George Blunt's simple question had caused such consternation.

It was nearly half an hour before the party began to break up. The two policemen were the first to make a move. As they did their round of *arrivedercis*, the younger one hesitated by my chair.

"I hope I shall see you again, Signorina Lyndon," he said politely. In a quieter voice he added: "And perhaps in less . . . formal circumstances."

Across the room, Giles scowled. He was getting just a little bit too possessive!

Devilry made me respond to Cesare Pastore more enthusiastically than I'd otherwise have done. "Perhaps we shall," I said brightly.

"Tomorrow?"

"Oh, but I'm afraid . . . "

I was saved the necessity of finding a let-out. Inspector Vigorelli came across and took his assistant's elbow.

"*Presto*, Cesare," he urged jocularly. "Life is not only for pleasure, young man. There is work to be done also."

With a fluid gesture conveying helpless resignation, Cesare moved away. But his expression told me he would be back, for sure.

As if to nail down a prior claim, Giles immediately rose to his feet and came over. The settee was small, and he was obliged to sit close. I shifted away an inch or two.

Cesare, on the point of leaving, raised his eyebrows. He was accepting Giles' implied challenge.

Almost as soon as the door was closed behind the two policemen, Signor Zampini asked Adeline: "Who is that fellow?"

"My dear Guido, you must have met Vigorelli before. He comes here often." She laughed with overdrawn modesty. "I know perfectly well, of course, that it is only because he likes to practise his English on me."

Zampini gestured impatiently. "It is the young one I ask about — the assistant."

"I know nothing about him except that he has just arrived in Sicily. This is the first time I have met him."

"Where does he come from?"

She shrugged. "From the North, I think he said. Milan, perhaps ... Why do you ask?"

Zampini chewed his lip thoughtfully. "It seems curious, to appoint a man who is not a Sicilian."

"Perhaps he applied for the post." Adeline laughed, and gave me an amused glance. "Would it be the climate that attracts him, do you suppose, or the beautiful girls?"

Aware that she had been neglecting her only real guests, the Yorkshire couple, Adeline switched every ounce of her considerable charm to them. Soon she had them talking eagerly. He boasted about the success of his woollen business in Halifax, and she of the way they spent the profits. Regretfully childless, it was obvious that they attempted to make good the deficiency by travelling and generally indulging themselves.

"My husband is quite an art collector," Rosalind said suddenly. Her remark was dropped into the conversational pool with studied casualness, almost as if she were announcing a connection with royalty.

Adeline pushed the tea wagon to one side before commenting: "How nice! And what period particularly interests you, Mr. Blunt?"

"Er ... I'm not fussy. If something takes my fancy, well then I'm willing to pay hard cash for it. I reckoned Italy was a good place to come."

"You will find less in Sicily than in Rome," Adeline pointed out. "But perhaps there is a good deal to see here."

George Blunt glanced swiftly from one to another of the many oil paintings on the walls of the salon. But Adeline shook her head.

"No, no. I meant in the art dealer's galleries."

In the briefest of pauses, I sensed something flash between Zampini and the Blunts. I was certain they had a secret understanding. But though I watched all three more closely from then on, I detected no outward sign of any inner tie.

"Happen you're right, my dear lady," George Blunt agreed, giving Adeline a nod of his balding head. "Rosie and I will be taking a good look around, anyhow."

I had to control my impatience a while longer before the Blunts departed upstairs. Then I drifted out of the room myself, manoeuvring to catch Adeline alone. I'd got to warn her about the strange collusion I suspected between her friend Zampini and the Yorkshire couple. I'd got to tell her that they most certainly had been acquainted before arriving at the *Villa d'Oro.*

To my annoyance, Giles followed me out. I got rid of him by saying I had work to do. Looking slightly nettled, he decided to go back to his studio. "I might as well get on with something myself."

"That wouldn't be a bad idea. You certainly don't seem to do overmuch work."

I'd spoken lightly, but immediately regretted my words. Giles leapt on them. "I could soon change all that, Kerry

darling," he said, looking uncharacter-
istically solemn. "It would be worth
working for you."

I felt embarrassed. "I was only joking."

"But I wasn't," he said softly. "I wasn't
joking a bit."

Luckily, he took himself off then. I
had a feeling I wouldn't have handled the
situation very well if he'd stuck around.

I still had to wait another fifteen
minutes before Adeline and Zampini
broke off their *tête-à-tête*, and he went
out to the loggia to find himself a
reclining chair.

I waylaid Adeline as she headed towards
the kitchen.

"I'd like to talk to you, Miss Harcourt."

"Is something wrong?"

I glanced around cautiously. Windows
and door were so often left wide open in
this climate.

"Perhaps we could go somewhere
private? It's rather . . . "

She hoisted her eyebrows. "Of course,
if you wish. Let's go up to my room."

I hadn't seen her private apartment
before. The furniture was simple and
white painted, but set off by fabrics in

strong, dramatic colours. It gave a total effect that was cool and restful, yet at the same time very much alive.

She went straight over and closed the windows. "There! Now we can talk without any possibility of being over heard. What is it, Kerry darling?"

I felt absurdly like a child coming to tell tales to teacher. "I think you ought to know that there's something odd going on between Signor Zampini and the Blunts. They're not strangers at all."

She looked faintly surprised. "What *do* you mean, darling?"

"Mr. Blunt said quite positively just now that they'd never met before. But they had. This morning, while I was out with Giles, I saw the three of them together in a restaurant."

Adeline was unperturbed. "But that's quite impossible, darling, Mr. and Mrs. Blunt arrived in Sicily only this afternoon."

"Miss Harcourt, you must believe me." I felt rather put out that she should doubt my word. "Don't forget that I met Signor Zampini before, in Rome." I risked offending by adding: "He is not difficult to recognise."

"It is possible that you saw Guido," she conceded. "He arrived in Sicily earlier, and might well have stopped off for a drink. But it must have been some other people he was talking to. The Blunts simply were not on the island then."

I nearly blurted out that I'd recognised Rosalind Blunt too, because I'd seen her once before. But that would have meant telling the details. I'd have to explain why, as I'd casually strolled past an hotel in Rome, I should have pinpointed a particular woman sitting at a terrace table.

"I'm quite certain that I am right," I said stubbornly. Adeline smiled and shook her head. "We all of us make mistakes sometimes, darling. But it was kind of you to tell me at once what you suspected. Now you can put the matter right out of your mind."

"But Miss Harcourt . . . "

"Just forget it, darling." There was a flatness in her voice that permitted no further argument.

Like handing out a consolation prize to a disappointed child, she went on to ask me to see to the dinner arrangements.

"Just keep a general eye on things. I shall be rather busy for a while."

There was in fact, very little to be done about dinner. When I went to the kitchen I found the plump Maria preparing a savoury stuffing for veal rolls. Her enormous arms trembled as she chopped herbs with a villainous-looking knife. On the draining board the vegetables were ready washed and waiting — onions, string beans, and the inevitable mountain of tomatoes. Maria had spent the time since siesta placidly working towards the evening meal.

I asked if there was anything I could do to help. She shook her head and grinned at me, showing gaps in her front teeth.

"No sank you, signorina. I am able." She spoke carefully, proud of her English.

In the dining-room Carlo was polishing wine glasses. His surliness hadn't softened one bit. He resented my presence at the *Stella d'Oro*, and although just managing to avoid unforgivable impertinence, he skated on remarkably thin ice.

"I understand very well how a table is laid, Miss Lyndon."

"You certainly do, Carlo." I was

determined to stay pleasant. "The whole room looks most attractive."

But my fulsome praise didn't help at all. His dark eyes were a damped-down fire. "I am surprised that you come to watch me, then."

To avoid an open row with him, I swallowed my anger and cleared out, leaving him to it. I went upstairs and got myself changed. I'd be more use, I reckoned, playing second-string hostess.

But that fell flat, too. Everybody seemed to be stuck in their rooms. I prowled around the empty salon, feeling thwarted.

When I heard a car scrunching up the drive, I thought it must be Giles again. But not for long. With a snap I remembered another guest was due to arrive today. How was this for a welcome? The deserted villa would strike him like a mausoleum.

I skipped back to the kitchen to dig out Carlo. He was sitting in a wickerwork chair with Luciana giggling on his lap. The girl jumped up when she saw me, but Carlo stayed put, his eyes boldly daring me to say something.

A split second inner debate decided me to let it go. But Carlo was none too pleased to be hauled off pronto to the front door.

We reached it just in time to see the car drawing up at the portico.

Carlo could rise to the occasion when he chose. He ran round and opened the car door with a flourish and a bow. The driver slid out and turned slowly to look up at the white façade of the villa.

But I knew before I saw the face. I knew by the swing of his shoulders, the jerk of his head as he nodded thanks to Carlo.

How could I fail to recognise an image etched so painfully deep?

It was Philip Rainsby.

5

HE was as startled as I was. We both stood rigid, staring at one another in disbelief.

Luckily, Carlo was too busy getting the bags out of the boot to notice our curious behaviour.

I said nothing. It was clearly a struggle for Philip to speak, and when he did, his words shook me still further.

"Good evening, Miss Lyndon."

Miss Lyndon! After all he had said to me in Rome. After those magic hours we had spent isolated together in the midst of the party din.

I still didn't speak. I *couldn't* speak. How long I might have stood there, gawping at him stupidly, I don't know. Mercifully, Miss Harcourt appeared from nowhere and came sweeping forward with a graciously welcoming smile.

"Good evening, Mr. Rainsby. You must forgive me for not being here to greet you, but I was . . . " She waved a vague hand, leaving him to guess what she meant. "But I see Kerry has already introduced herself. Do come in."

She led the way across the hall. "I see you've hired a car. *Such* a good idea, otherwise you might feel rather cut off in this remote part of the world. But aren't those dusty roads simply beyond anything? You'll be wanting to freshen up, I'm sure, and when you're ready, I hope you will join the rest of us for cocktails before dinner . . . "

The flow of her words was undiminished as she piloted him up the stairs. I was left gazing after them.

What a ghastly coincidence that Philip should turn up here — just as I was getting him out of my system. And then to have him treat me so coldly, as if there had never been that *magnetism* between us!

In these past few days I'd made myself believe that Philip had merely been amusing himself with me at a tedious party; that it had all meant nothing to him. But if I really and truly accepted that, why this crushing despair at his snub?

Miss Lyndon!

There must have been a small chink of hope left that I'd got it all wrong. A chink that had sprung wide open at the sight of him here.

But now the door was closed and locked and bolted. There could never be forgiveness enough in my heart to open it again.

Miss Lyndon!

I wanted to run away and hide. Wild notions rushed through my head about quitting the *Stella d'Oro* here and now. I just couldn't bear the idea of sleeping under the same roof as Philip Rainsby.

I had enough money to get back to England. Though I'd refused Monica's over-generous offer of six month's salary in lieu of notice, she had still insisted on giving me what she called a tiny golden handshake.

Back home, I could dodge the problem of facing up to Philip Rainsby. Engulfed in the anonymity of London, there would be no likelihood of ever meeting up with him again.

The urge to get out and lick my hurt in private was almost overwhelming. But

I fought it and won. No man on earth was going to be allowed that much power over my emotions!

The Blunts had come downstairs, slicked up ready for dinner. Rosalind was wearing a white nylon gown threaded through with silver. Her mass of shining blonde hair was looped so it fell in a sexy swag across her left shoulder. She had good looks. But they weren't the looks of eighteen. She should dress her age, I thought sourly.

But in George Blunt's eyes I bet she was everything he wanted of his wife. He had the adoring look of a middle-aged husband successfully led by the nose.

I used the pair of them to prove I was still in command of myself. When Adeline came downstairs I was chatting in top gear.

Choosing the moment, I tossed in my bombshell, watching Rosalind's face for whatever it might betray.

"Mr. Rainsby has just arrived, so he'll be with us for dinner."

To my surprise she merely nodded and smiled. Her husband too said something about it being right champion.

"A good lad, is Philip."

So they had known he was coming — both of them! I'd doubted if George Blunt would so much as recognise the name.

Adeline rang for Carlo to serve drinks. "So you know Mr. Rainsby, then?"

"Aye, we know young Philip all right."

"We met him in Rome," explained Rosalind demurely. "In fact, it was after we mentioned about staying here that he decided to come. I'm glad you were able to find room for him."

I'll bet you were, I thought grimly. How nice and easy, in this remote spot, to carry on an undercover affair. And stupid trusting old George all unsuspecting!

Acute surprise had fleeted across Adeline's face. I had a feeling she was disturbed about something she couldn't understand. But her recovery towards poise was swift.

"How very pleasant that you are friends already."

A few minutes later Philip joined us, and greeted the Blunts warmly. I gave him a frozen nod, and he seemed more than ready to preserve the tone of his distant first greeting.

We all wandered out through wideflung windows to the loggia. The cooling evening air was heavy with a scent of jasmine from the trellised stone canopy above us.

It could have been utterly delightful. But in fact none of us except George Blunt seemed to be in any mood to enjoy such tranquilly beautiful surroundings. An elusive tension hung in the atmosphere.

Rosalind Blunt seemed eager to demonstrate there was nothing beyond the most trivial link between herself and Philip. She was laughing and talking vivaciously, making sure the whole party was included in every remark. It contrasted oddly with her behaviour at afternoon tea. Then, she'd had very little to say for herself, until Adeline had skilfully encouraged her.

Adeline's usual smooth command of any situation had deserted her now. She seemed uneasy and apprehensive, as if she was expecting something unpleasant to happen.

A shadow fell across the light streaming out from the salon. Guido Zampini's grotesque figure almost filled the width of the doors. He was staring blankly at Philip.

"*You*, Rainsby?"

Philip strolled over. "Good evening, Signor Zampini. I didn't expect to see you here."

The Italian seemed too bewildered to take Philip's outstretched hand. "Myself, I did not expect you."

"But surely it was . . . " Philip stopped abruptly, and then began again. "I thought I mentioned to you that I was coming over."

"Yes. But not so soon, I understood."

Philip frowned. "Does it matter? It's nice to meet you again, anyway."

Zampini recollected himself, and made a plainly false effort to be jovial. "Of course, my friend, of course. It is delightful to find you here, I assure you."

Adeline had disappeared inside, and now came out with a drink for Zampini. "So you two know one another as well. But how very nice!"

Zampini grabbed the glass without a word of thanks. He was glaring at Adeline angrily. "I must speak with you."

"Later, Guido."

"No, *now!*" It reminded me of the spiteful hissing of a snake.

Adeline's smile became strained at the edges. "I said *later*, Guido." She wafted over to George and Rosalind Blunt and involved herself in conversation with them.

Baffled, Zampini glowered after her.

When we went in for dinner, the party was split up at tables for two. The Blunts were close to Adeline and me. The timid little Austrian couple slipped in, smiling nervously, and scurried over to their alcove table.

Philip and Zampini were placed together across the room, and were immediately deep in conversation. They spoke in undertones inaudible to the rest of us. Whenever Carlo went to serve them, they seemed to dry up until he had gone away again.

Maria had produced another superb dinner. My spirit of defiance gave me the appetite to do it justice. I certainly wasn't going to let Philip think his presence here had thrown me.

We all came together again for coffee in the salon. The moment that was through, Adeline went off with Zampini. They didn't appear again for some time, not until I had done my checkup rounds in kitchen and dining-room.

I felt certain there had been a flaming row. Adeline looked pale but determined. Zampini still looked angry. All in all, the rest of the evening promised to be darned uncomfortable.

Playing hostess like mad, Adeline tried to make up a Bridge four. But her efforts fell flat. Whilst George Blunt was keen enough, his wife decided she just didn't feel like it tonight. Philip begged off by making out he was a goof at cards. I had to duck out because I was utterly hopeless. In the end Adeline had to settle for Solo Whist with Zampini and George Blunt.

As if casually, Philip and Rosalind Blunt were talking together. They were sitting near enough to the card party not to cause any speculations, yet far enough away to be out of earshot.

Philip didn't once look in my direction.

If I'd been a guest myself, I'd have left them to it. But I couldn't very well do that. I felt obliged to hang about where I might be needed. So I just sat idly watching the card players, wishing Giles was around. Since he normally spent so much time at the villa, why did he have to choose this evening to stay away?

I thought for a second he had turned up after all when a tall figure appeared at one of the windows. But then I recognised Cesare Pastore, the police chief's assisant.

He took a diffident step inside, and bowed to Adeline.

"Forgive my intrusion, Signora, but I was wondering . . . "

She first gave him a nice ordinary friendly smile, and then switched to being the gracious lady amused by his confusion.

"Yes, young man? What was it you were wondering?"

"I thought Signorina Lyndon might perhaps care to come with me for a drive. It is a beautiful evening."

Adeline was already studying her cards again, thoughtfully smoothing her upswept hair. "Yes, yes. You go with him, Kerry darling."

"But . . . " I began.

"Be off with you." The single finger she wagged above her head conveyed a playful admonishment. "And not too late back with her, my young friend. Remember!"

Though I'd been longing to escape from the insufferable atmosphere of the salon, I objected to the way I was being organised. Adeline was practically ordering me to go. But Cesare, having gained her approval, then proceeded to invite me most flatteringly.

"I should be very happy if you would consent to come with me for a drive. Please signorina, do say you will."

Zampini said heavily, and loud enough for everyone to hear: "I do not think it is right . . . "

"Not right for young people to enjoy themselves?" cried Adeline gaily. "Nonsense, my dear Guido. You forget your own youth."

But what really made up my mind was the sight of Philip across the room. He was watching me sullenly, his face set into lines of deep ill-humour.

"I'd love to come," I said quickly. "Just hang on a minute, while I fetch a coat."

"I will be waiting . . . outside in my

automobile." Cesare gave a charming smile. But he must have sensed that the general mood was not in his favour. Guido had made an unwarranted objection to my going out at all; Philip was now scowling fiercely. Rosalind Blunt looked none too pleased either, but that, I guessed, was because Philip's attention had been diverted from her.

It was a glorious evening, the landscape etched sharp by a nearly full moon. As we drove off I looked towards Etna, and saw the great snow-streaked cone flaring with a weird inner light of its own.

Cesare's car bore no resemblance to Gile's slick sports model. It was more like the one Philip had hired, a sober little black job. I guessed it was an official police car, borrowed for the evening.

We drove along deserted roads. The sleeping countryside looked tranquilly beautiful.

When I said as much to Cesare his reply was sombre. "This is not a tranquil island, Kerry. Throughout history life has been hard for Sicilians. And it still is . . . "

"I read all about the terrible earthquake."

He was silent for a moment before saying quietly, "Yes, that too . . . "

He spoke fluently and colloquially, making hardly any errors even in pronunciation.

"How come your English is so marvellous?" I asked.

"Oh . . . we took it at school, you know."

"Maybe. But yours is far above school level, surely?"

"Ah well — I have kept it up. Languages are useful to a policeman."

"In Sicily?"

"Here, as everywhere else."

I couldn't help liking Cesare. Apart from the fact that he was a darned attractive man by any standards, his unaffected chivalry was extremely fetching. He was so thoroughly nice that I began to feel guilty about my reasons for accepting his invitation. I had to face it — basically I'd just wanted to get one back at Philip.

"What was it that brought you to Sicily?" Cesare asked. "Did you think that to work in the sun would make a nice change from an English hotel?"

"Oh, but I've never done anything like this before. It was quite by chance that I took a job here."

I told him about Monica, and her sudden decision to marry Sam Tracy and live in the United States.

"Monica Halliday-Browne?" he said in a ruminative voice. "I cannot recollect ever hearing that name before."

"There's no reason why you should have done. She's hardly a celebrity, even though she gets around an awful lot."

"So it seems. Quite the cosmopolitan, it appears. Always on the move."

I shrugged. "Monica is one of those restless souls. I don't think her sort ever know what it is they want out of life."

"Perhaps you are right. Or it could be that they know very well?"

"I don't get you."

He pulled the little car round a sweeping bend, and revved away again.

"Just an idle remark," he said carelessly. "It must have been a shock for you when Monica Halliday-Browne announced she was leaving Italy."

"I was pretty fed up. I didn't want to

go back to England so soon."

"What did you do, then?"

"Luckily Monica thought of Miss Harcourt, who happened to be in Rome at the time. I was fixed up with this job within a couple of hours."

"Quick work! And what precisely is your job, if I may ask?"

Putting it into words was difficult. "I'm expected to help Miss Harcourt generally any way I can."

"But you find there is not enough for you to do, in fact?"

He'd touched a sore spot, and I reacted with swift annoyance. I didn't like the idea of anyone else considering my job a sinecure.

Cesare stopped the car abruptly, and turned to me. "I am so sorry if I have offended you. But Miss Harcourt herself said you were complaining."

"Yes, of course. I'd forgotten that."

He settled more comfortably in his seat, and took out cigarettes. I refused one, but told him to go ahead.

"See old Mother Etna," he said, pointing. "She is angry tonight."

As we watched the mountain, belches

of denser smoke were thrown up, blood-tinged against the moonlit sky. Etna looked like a gigantic smouldering bonfire. A shudder gripped me at the thought of the volcano's destructive potential.

"Is it often like this?"

I felt Cesare's shrug where his shoulders touched mine. "She has her ups and downs, like all of us Italians."

"I don't get the impression that you are a particularly eruptive type," I said with truth. "You seem to be very level-headed."

"Aha, but I have my moments. Especially . . . " he swung round, half facing me, "especially with an attractive woman."

In what I hoped was a neat sidestep, I said: "I hope Etna doesn't get really worked up while I am in Sicily."

He laughed. "Are English girls always so cautious?"

"Only when the necessity arises."

Still laughing, he reached forward and flicked on the ignition.

We stopped somewhere for a drink, and then Cesare drove me back to the *Stella d'Oro.* He asked if he could see me again soon. "Perhaps you will allow me to take you out to dinner?"

"Thanks, I'd like that."

"Then I will telephone." He clicked his heels and bowed in a parody of his chief's Latin gallantry. But the kiss he pressed on the back of my hand was not entirely a joke.

"Goodnight, Kerry ... " His voice lingered over my name.

When I walked into the salon I was no longer thinking of Philip Rainsby. I had gone out with Cesare to spite Philip, and had ended up by having fun.

Only two people were there now – Adeline Harcourt and Zampini. The Italian scowled at me, thick black eyebrows almost meeting over his big nose.

Adeline still seemed very much on edge as she asked: "Did you have a pleasant evening, darling?"

"Yes thank you, Miss Harcourt."

She hesitated, then plunged in with what sounded remarkably like a prepared speech. "Kerry – I feel I should warn you. That young man may seem very nice, but a friendship with him could be dangerous . . . "

"Dangerous? How do you mean?"

"You must remember he is Italian — and far away from his own home. Besides, we have heard things . . . rumours. I advise you not to let yourself be alone with him again."

I felt a surge of anger. "And just what rumours have you heard about Cesare?" I asked in a stiffly restrained voice.

"Never mind. You are young . . . "

"I am not a child, Miss Harcourt."

Guido Zampini lumbered out of his armchair and came towards me, scowling. "You will listen to Miss Harcourt. She speaks as she does only because she has your best interests in her heart."

I didn't answer him. If I had tried to, the strand holding my temper would certainly have snapped. Instead I addressed Miss Harcourt again. I tried to be reasonable in face of this quite unreasonable interference in my private affairs.

"You are making far too much of a perfectly ordinary incident," I said with care. "I've been for a drive with Cesare. And that is all. Another time I may have dinner with him."

"That would be madness," thundered Zampini. "I forbid you to do any such thing."

"Will you kindly mind your own business," I blazed. "What I may do or may not do isn't the smallest concern of yours."

"Tell the imbecile, Adeline," snapped Zampini. "If she won't listen to me, then *you* tell her."

Before Miss Harcourt could speak again, I gave her fair warning.

"It had better be understood right now," I said in a level voice, "that how I occupy myself when I'm off duty is entirely my own affair. I have no wish to be disrespectful, Miss Harcourt, but you have no right to interfere in my private life."

If she fired me on the spot, that was all right by me. But I was darned if I'd stand for this, from her, or from anyone else.

6

I DIDN'T hang around for Adeline's comeback. I stalked out of the salon and straight upstairs, flaming with indignation.

By bad luck, just as I reached the landing outside my bedroom door I ran into Philip. We both of us stopped, six feet apart. Our eyes met and held.

For a brief instant something flickered between us, piercing the formal skin we'd plastered over our relationship. We acknowledged the intensity of caring that had sprung up between us in Rome. And then the contact was broken. A look of cold indifference settled on Philip's face again.

I dived for the shelter of my room. My pent-up emotions were too much for me, and I felt like slamming the door violently. But just in time I held back. It cost me a tone of self-control to close the door gently. Then I went over and switched on the transistor. If

Philip was still hanging around outside, let him make what he could of the sound of cheerful pop music from Naples.

A full hour must have passed before I even made a start to go to bed. I spent the time idly padding around the room, hugging my misery. As if it wasn't bad enough to have Philip about the place, now I had a grievance against Adeline Harcourt.

The unfairness of her attitude hit me hard. She had pressed me to go for a drive with Cesare, practically ordered me to, in fact. And then, barely a couple of hours afterwards, she tried to make out it was rash of me to be friendly with him, hinting vaguely at sordid rumours.

As for Zampini daring to intervene! To have the sheer nerve to boss me around!

It struck me that Adeline's about-turn was Zampini's responsibility. He'd objected before I went, and although Adeline had overridden him then, he must have argued her round.

That man had an unhealthy influence over Adeline. I was convinced of it. However much she protested they were old friends, I couldn't believe she would free-willingly choose to be so thick with such an unpleasant character.

It was a puzzle, though, why Zampini should care one way or the other about my going out with Cesare. For that matter, why should he care two straws whatever I did? But for some reason he had it in for me, and I didn't fool myself any longer it was merely because I'd once snubbed him.

A recollection shot into my mind. That first time I'd met Adeline, she had been speaking to someone on the phone. I dug into my memory for the exact words. Something about just a little help with the domestic arrangements, and of no consequence to *us* . . .

Was it Guido Zampini she'd been talking to?

What a fool not to have realised at the time she was referring to me. Of course it was me! And I might have questioned just who it was she'd got to placate, since the guesthouse belonged to her. But my mind had been too ravaged by the sight of Philip and that Blunt woman, intimately gay on a hotel terrace.

And hadn't Adeline also said something

like '*there is no earthly reason why she should ever find out*'?

I'd certainly been a fool all right. A fool not to have been suspicious. A fool to have jumped slap-happily into this blind date of a job.

By morning I had decided to quit. The row over Cesare finally pinpointed the absurdity of my position here. There was no question of leaving Adeline in the lurch, for clearly I wasn't really needed at all. I'd owe her nothing — nothing but a certain gratitude for having offered me a job out of sheer kindness of heart.

Philip Rainsby, I told myself, was entirely unconnected with my decision. I had at last achieved indifference towards him. Whether he stayed or not, whether he acknowledged me or not, was neither here nor there.

I was downstairs by eight, and to my surprise found Adeline there ahead of me. She took the belligerent wind out of my sails by apologising.

"I must beg you to forgive me, Kerry darling. What I said last night was unpardonable." She looked at me with candidly respectful eyes. "I admire your spirit in telling me straight out that I am nothing but an interfering old woman."

"But I didn't say that, Miss Harcourt . . . "

Her mobile lips pursed in amusement. "Damn nearly, though! And so I am. And now I'm asking you to forgive me for it."

From standing there tall and erect, she once again seemed to shrink into tremulous frailty. It was a mirage, I knew. Or rather, a superb piece of acting.

Her pose made it more difficult to announce my decision. And we were still standing at the foot of the stairs; I was uneasily aware that one of the guests might appear at any moment.

I took the plunge. "Miss Harcourt, I've been thinking. I know it was terribly kind of you to give me this job, but . . . well, we both know there isn't any job really . . . "

The old lady image slipped out of focus as Adeline asked sharply: "What do you mean by that?"

"Only what I've said before — there's not enough for me to do with so few guests staying here."

"It is possible I may decide to take

more guests later on. In the meantime, surely it's enough to know that I want you."

"I really don't see why you should."

"Please stay, Kerry. *Please!*"

There was an intensity about her appeal that astonished me. For an instant I thought I saw fear in her eyes. Then she looked away, and was at once so much in command of herself that I felt sure I'd imagined the fear.

Adeline kept silent for a moment. She was watching me shrewdly, as if trying to get under my skin.

Suddenly, right out of the blue, she asked quietly: "Had you met Philip Rainsby before he came here?"

"*No!*"

The lie was on my tongue before I'd worked out the reason for it. Caught on the hop, my reply was blind instinct, a defensive reaction. If I admitted I had known Philip, she would ask more questions. I didn't want that; the hurt was too deep.

"No," I reaffirmed with more stability. "Why do you ask?"

"It was the way you were looking at

one another when he first arrived."

So Adeline had noticed my moments of stunned surprise at Philip's turning up here. I'd been kidding myself she'd seen nothing.

Foolishly, I was committed; I could hardly go back on that emphatic denial now. She would think me mad if I told her: "Well . . . actually we did meet in Rome . . . " So I too would have to join in the ridiculous game of pretence. Well, if the Blunts and Zampini could keep it up, then I could too.

I tried to shrug lightly. "I can't imagine what could have given you the impression that we knew one another."

Adeline dismissed the matter with a little no-consequence smile, and briskly disappeared into the salon. Delighted to escape her probing, it was some time before I realised that the question of my leaving had been forgotten.

Or had it? Maybe the diversion about Philip was a stratagem to get me off a subject she wished to avoid.

Somehow I was curiously hesitant about raising it again. I couldn't forget Adeline's almost desperate entreaty — "Please stay,

Kerry — *please!*" I couldn't forget that fleeting look of fear which I still wasn't certain I had really seen at all.

I felt myself trapped by circumstance at the *Villa Stella d'Oro.* There was really nothing tangible to stop me going away — right back to England if I felt like it. Yet I couldn't bring myself to take that step. I was stuck here for the time being.

To make matters worse, I was in the absurd position of having denied all previous knowledge of Philip Rainsby. Still, with Philip so aloof, there was mighty little danger of him blowing the gaff about our meeting in Rome.

But in comforting myself, I was entirely overlooking a vital fact. Philip and I had met at a party given by Guido Zampini. He must have seen us together.

Resigned to staying on, I determined that as of now I'd take a real hand in the running of the *Stella d'Oro.* And if Adeline didn't like it that way she could either lump it, or fire me.

In this new tough mood, I sailed through to the kitchen. I'd already discovered that domestic arrangements at the villa were not quite so perfect as they'd appeared at first sight. Now I noticed a breakfast tray of coffee and rolls waiting on the dresser. The coffee pot was barely warm.

"Whose is this?" I asked abruptly.

Carlo didn't even trouble to reply. But Maria, in her usual placid way, told me it was for the honeymooners. They always breakfasted in their room.

"Then why hasn't it been taken up to them?"

Carlo regarded me with deep dislike. "I am busy."

I swung back to his aunt. "Please make fresh coffee, Maria and then Carlo will take the tray upstairs *immediately*. Is that understood?"

I enjoyed the next couple of hours. It was great to be really occupied again. I realised now that I'd been missing out on that sort of satisfaction ever since leaving Dr. Stewart. Monica had been fun, but never for a single moment had she taken work seriously.

Everything I delved into except the cooking itself was wide open for improvement. After a huddle in the storeroom,

Maria and I agreed on several ways of cutting waste. I felt convinced that Carlo was up to his neck in petty fiddles. That young man was in for a mighty big shock!

About eleven I started on the flowers, a job I had already made my own. With all that fabulous colour rioting in the garden, it seemed a pity not to bring some of it indoors. The old gardener and I were fast friends, even though our conversation was limited to my few words of Italian. Pietro kept me supplied with all the blooms I needed.

The little utility room off the hall smelled like heaven. Pietro's lavish offering for the day stood all around me in buckets of cool water. Opposite, through the salon's open doors, I could glimpse Adeline and the Blunts. They seemed to be doing a tour of the room and after a while I realised they were discussing the paintings.

"My soul demands beauty," I heard Adeline say in her carrying voice. "I must be surrounded by lovely things."

I grinned to myself as I fixed a vase of madonna lilies. From anyone else such high-flown sentiment would sound like humbug, but Adeline could get away with it.

George Blunt's voice boomed. "You're a lucky woman to own such a grand house, Miss Harcourt. Happen you've been here long?"

"Just over fifteen years," she told him. "But of course the *Stella d'Oro* has been in my family for *generations*. It was built by an ancestor of mine a couple of centuries ago."

"Was he English?" queried Rosalind.

"No, no. I have a *soupçon* of Sicilian blood in my veins. The villa remained in the hands of the Italian branch of the family until quite recently . . . "

In sheer astonishment I stopped working on the flowers. I was trying to reconcile this story with what Adeline had told me on the plane. She'd said then, and without wrapping it up, that the *Villa Stella d'Oro* had been a gift from her lover.

Just who was she trying to impress — me or the Blunts? And why, for goodness' sake, tell lies to either of us?

Maybe Adeline's flamboyant nature

demanded a background suited to her immediate audience. Maybe she thought that the romantic tale of an Italian lover would be fascinating to me. The Blunts, however — *nouveaux riches* from stolid Yorkshire, would be more likely to go for an ancient family home with English and Italian roots.

And the funny thing was, I didn't hold it against her one bit. If she spun a different tale to everyone she met, good luck to her! With Adeline Harcourt it wasn't a matter of 'lying'; just that she was always on-stage.

"You've got a lot of grand paintings here," George Blunt was saying. "Right champion, I reckon."

Adeline accepted the compliment modestly. "They are nice, aren't they?"

"One or two of 'em I wouldn't mind having myself. No, I wouldn't mind at all!" There was a pause, as if he was studying a picture more closely. Then I heard him say: "Ever think of selling?"

"Sell my paintings! Good heavens no, I should never sell any of these. They are far too precious." She sighed wistfully. "Of course, I know they aren't terribly valuable, but it's the . . . the sentimental associations, you see."

"That's very understandable."

"Having been part of my life for so many years, I feel that our destinies are bound up together." Through the two doorways I caught the glint of her silver hair as she shook her head decidedly. "No, Mr. Blunt, I don't think I could ever bring myself to dispose of any of the paintings in here."

"Happen you've got some others that aren't quite so precious to you," George Blunt suggested. "As my Rosie told you, I'm quite a collector in a modest sort of way. Always ready to offer a fair price, cash down, for something that takes my fancy."

Rosalind chipped in: "George is always saying to me, 'Never mind your old masters', he says. 'If I like a thing, that's good enough for me'."

"How very sensible of him," agreed Adeline. "Too few people these days dare trust their own judgement."

She hadn't taken up George Blunt's hint, and he repeated it.

"If you've got any other paintings

knocking around, Miss Harcourt, happen I'd like to take a look at them."

Adeline seemed not much interested. "There might be one or two, I suppose. As a matter of fact, I believe there are some put away in the attics, though I've hardly been up there myself for years."

"Could I have a look at them, do you reckon?"

Adeline sounded faintly amused by his persistence. "If you really want to, Mr. Blunt, I'll show you sometime."

"There's no time like the present, I always say."

"I'm sorry," she said flatly, "but I've got far too much to see to just now. Anyway, there's no hurry."

The flowers were finished. I carried an urn of tall delphinium spikes through to the salon.

Adeline and the Blunts had been talking without restraint but at the sight of me they dried up abruptly. It was as if, by mutual consent, the subject of pictures had been dropped like a hot potato. George Blunt blustered a fatuous remark about the pretty flowers, and his wife and Adeline eagerly jumped aboard the bandwagon. They were still all fervently discussing flowers when I left the room.

At noon I was checking the dining-room tables when Giles stuck his head round the door.

"Well well, what a busy little bee you are, then."

"Hallo, Giles. Have you come for lunch?"

"Is that an invitation, Kerry darling?"

"It is not an invitation. I just want to know whether to have an extra place laid for you."

His wide grin took on a rueful twist. "And here was I fondly imagining you wanted the pleasure of my company."

Discovering that two of the pepper pots were empty, I gathered them up to show Carlo. "It's for Miss Harcourt to ask you to stay to lunch, Giles, not me."

"Oh, Adeline won't mind," he said carelessly. "What about this afternoon, Kerry?"

"What about it?"

"Would you like to come to my studio and see some of my paintings?"

I flickered him an ironical glance. "Are you sure you don't mean your etchings?"

"Now that really would be something!"

Opening the door to the kitchen, I handed the pepper pots to Carlo for filling.

Giles asked again. "Will you, Kerry?"

"What? Come to your studio?"

"Uhuh."

So far I'd not been taking him seriously, just idly back-chatting. "Not today, Giles. I really am too busy."

"You can't be — not at siesta time."

"Oh, I'm not bothered about that." I'd planned to go through the linen room upstairs. From what I'd seen it badly needed clearing out.

"Don't be daft, Kerry," he said explosively. "There's people whose job it is to look after that sort of thing."

"And it's my job to see they do," I slung back. "Make it tomorrow, will you? I'd like to come then — just for a little while."

Giles stayed at the villa for lunch, easily wangling an invitation out of Adeline. But he wasn't successful in getting me to change my mind about going back to Taormina with him. He went off round about three, none too pleased with life.

The linen room was certainly in a mess. I decided to make a start by chucking out an accumulation of junk which had been pushed to the back. I fetched a big cardboard box from downstairs, and filled it with bits and pieces — chipped vases, copper hot water cans, and some ancient oil lamps. With as much as I could carry in one load, I tottered through to the rear of the house, and started up the attic stairs.

At this time of day everything was deathly still. The villa was in semi-darkness, shutters closed against the scorching heat outside.

I could hear a low murmur of voices, and guessed it must be the Blunts resting in their room. I could just detect a Yorkshire brogue in the man's deep voice, though I couldn't decipher what he was saying.

Wedging my load against the wall at the top of the stairs, I made a random choice of the door on the right, throwing it wide open.

The room was not empty, as I had confidently expected. Adeline and the Blunts stood in a tight-knit group, facing me, gawping their eyes out. In the moment before George Blunt took a sly sideways step, I caught sight of a painting propped on the table behind them.

Adeline was first to recover composure. "What do *you* want?" she asked coldly, omitting that almost inevitable 'Kerry darling'.

"I was just bringing up this box of oddments to get them out of the way," I said, cross at being thrown on to the defensive.

"Oh . . . oh I see." But Adeline's voice was still freezing. "Well, put it down, girl. Just put it down anywhere."

It was as if she had only just managed to check herself from adding: '*And be off with you*'. Her urgent desire to get rid of me was patently clear.

Dumping the box on the floor, I backed out. "I do apologise for butting in . . . "

"Nonsense! We were only . . . " Adeline was full of scorn; but she didn't finish the sentence.

Closing the door behind me, I skipped down the steep staircase.

The whole episode had me guessing. Although I'd overheard George Blunt asking to see the paintings in the attic, I was amazed that Adeline should be showing them to him now, at siesta time. She made it such a rigid rule to rest each afternoon, declaring herself completely Sicilian in this respect.

There was no doubt at all that my sudden appearance had shaken all three of them. George and Rosaline Blunt had kept their worried eyes clamped right on me, though they hadn't uttered a single word. They gave the impression of being caught in the act.

But what act? Could it be they were trying to put one across a simple old lady? Maybe they were hoping to pick up a valuable painting for a song, because Adeline didn't know any better.

But I couldn't fit Adeline Harcourt into this handy bit of theorising. She was intelligent, a woman of wide worldly knowledge. She was also very shrewd, I was sure of that. And anyway, Adeline had been just as bothered as the Blunts when I'd blundered in on them.

I just didn't catch on. For the next hour, as I worked in the stifling heat of the small linen room, I kept chewing it over. But when I'd finished the job, I was no nearer a solution of the mystery. Nothing made any sense.

By the time the company assembled for afternoon tea Adeline was her usual elegantly charming self. Everyone was there. Zampini, in a tight-stretched suit, sweating sullenly. Giles, in white shirt and lightweight slacks, coolly tried to hold my eye. The Blunts were oddly reserved, even George keeping his mouth shut and smiling at everyone with obvious artificiality. The Austrian honeymooners sat away across the room, close to one another, and as far from the rest of us as possible.

And Philip. It seemed mighty odd to me, the way he'd hung around the villa all day. I'd have expected him to be off on a sightseeing trip.

But what Philip Rainsby did, or what he didn't, was no business of mine. I wasn't even interested.

Adeline, serenely playing the grand lady, dispensed tea from the chased silver pot and led the conversation where fancy took her.

As the talk flowered, I thought what a

false assemblage we were! The Blunts and Zampini, making out they didn't know one another; and Philip and I pretending the same thing. Adeline, lying in her teeth to the Blunts, or me or both, about how she came to acquire the *Villa Stella d'Oro.* And then there was this thing between Philip and Rosalind Blunt.

Was anything in this darned place on the level?

7

CURIOSITY got the better of me. When tea was over I waylaid Adeline on the stairs.

"Miss Harcourt," I began contritely. "I'm awfully sorry about this afternoon."

"What are you referring to, Kerry darling?"

"I mean, bursting in on you like that."

I was watching her closely, trying to read her expression. But she gave nothing away.

"My dear child, it is not of the slightest consequence. What could have made you think it mattered?"

"I thought . . . well, I got the idea you were displeased." She shook her head emphatically. "Of course not. I was delighted you were making yourself so useful." Standing with her hand on the banister rail, she paused thoughtfully. I imagined she was going to explain the scene in the attic, but I was quite mistaken. She shot out suddenly: "Perhaps

I could ask you not to take your duties quite so ... *enthusiastically.* You see, darling, Carlo has been complaining ... "

"Carlo? I don't get it."

"He feels ... Now you must not misunderstand this, Kerry darling, but these Sicilians can be very touchy at times. He imagines you are being over fussy about the way he does his work."

It riled me that Carlo should go running to Miss Harcourt. It astonished me that she should even listen to his whining.

"I assure you that nothing I said to Carlo was unjustified."

She put a placating hand on my arm. "I am quite certain you did not mean it to be, darling."

"You see ... " I fumbled, trying to find the right words. I wanted to avoid sounding critical of the way Adeline had been running the villa; or rather, of the way she had been letting it run itself. "Maybe you've not had time for the close supervision I can give things now."

The cautious approach hadn't worked. Her pained expression was slightly larger than life-size.

111

"You are probably right. I am an old woman."

"But I didn't mean . . . " Oh hell! I thought angrily. It's a simple enough thing to say. That Carlo had been getting away with murder, nearly; cheating her left, right and centre, and wasting far too much of his working time fooling around with Luciana.

Finally I said: "If you leave Carlo to me, I think it won't be long before he knuckles under and begins to co-operate."

"But he's a valuable servant, darling."

"Surely that's no excuse for slacking?"

"It would be difficult to replace him."

I doubted that Carlo was likely to quit such a soft job. He knew when he was on to a good thing.

"I just happen to think he ought to give fair measure when he's treated so well."

"All the same, darling," said Adeline decidedly, "you had better not criticise him any more. If you find him skimping his work, then you must come to me. I will take it up with him myself."

"But Miss Harcourt, I'm supposed to be here as your assistant — to take some

112

of the work off your shoulders."

"And that is exactly what you *are* doing, darling; you're an enormous help. But I ask you not to say anything more to upset Carlo."

Adeline turned and sailed up the stairs, making a majestic exit from the stage. I began to feel I was taking part in a farce.

Boiling inside, I went back to the salon. By bad luck Carlo was on the ball for once, already piling cups and saucers on the tea wagon. The grin he gave me high-lighted his malevolence. I was certain he knew Adeline had ticked me off about him. Maybe he had even overheard our conversation.

When he had finished clearing away, he asked meekly: "Is everything to the Signorina's entire satisfaction?"

I flatly refused to let him get under my skin. Unhurried, I glanced around. "Yes, thank you, Carlo. I think that's the lot."

Pushing the wagon, he headed for the door. Carlo was not all that subtle, though. I could tell from his discomfited walk he'd been cheated of the total victory he had played for.

After dinner the *Stella d'Oro* settled into its usual torpid state.

Philip wasn't the only one with no taste for sightseeing. The Blunts too had just hung around the villa all day, Rosalind looking bored stiff most of the time. For all her husband's alleged interest in art, they hadn't exactly fallen over themselves to see the glories of Sicily.

I couldn't understand why they were staying at the *Stella d'Oro.* They'd have been far happier at a snazzy hotel in Palermo or Taormina, where there was more going on. Some night life.

And the same applied to Philip. A remote villa lost in the hills seemed hardly the ideal place for a man on his own. I could only assume he found Rosalind Blunt so attractive that she was worth chasing anywhere.

When the police chief dropped in around nine, a Bridge four was made up — Adeline, Zampini, George Blunt and Inspector Vigorelli.

Rosalind sat alone on a sofa, irritably flicking through magazines she quite obviously wasn't reading. Dear Rosie looked thoroughly fed-up, and I knew why! Philip had gone upstairs. I went over and tried to make polite conversation — after all, she was a guest. But for my pains I got short answers and a total lack of interest, so I gave up.

For lack of anything else to do, I began listening to the card players. Zampini had just made a remark in Italian.

The police inspector nodded discreetly in George Blunt's direction. "Should we not speak English, Signor Zampini?"

Adeline's chuckle had malicious overtones. "That is the only reason you come here, Inspector — to practise your English upon us."

"But signora . . . !!" Expressive hands, splayed playing cards and all, were held up in horrified protest.

Zampini was entirely unamused. Stolidly, he tried again, this time speaking in English. "It is odd that a man from the North should come here as your assistant."

Very deliberately, the inspector played a card before replying. "Why should you think it odd, signore?"

"Surely it is unusual?"

The mobile shoulders shrugged. "I

think not. In any event, I am glad he is come. Cesare Pastore is a very ... a very promising young policeman."

"He is not with you tonight?"

"He is busy." Laughing, the inspector added: "It is right that the young should work and the old should relax, eh?"

Adeline, partnering George Blunt, frowned at her cards, and there was a general silence until she had played. Then, with a triumphant flourish, Zampini slapped down his card, and looked round for approval. But doggedly, he still pursued his evident interest in Cesare.

"And is your young friend on the track of some criminal desperado?"

The inspector regarded him blandly. "I think, signore, you have played the wrong suit." He glanced at the other two questioningly. "We will let him take it back, yes, as this is only a friendly game?"

Scowling blackly, Zampini snatched up the trespassing card. His question was not repeated.

I was bored. Once again I found myself wishing Giles were here. Hanging around in the daytime he got in my way, but he certainly enlivened the rather sedate atmosphere of the *Villa Stella d'Oro.* Giles would have been fun right now.

Or even Cesare Pastore. He'd have been company of my own age group. That, I told myself, was what I lacked.

I couldn't settle to reading, though I had an exciting book on the go. Very down in the dumps, I slipped quietly out of the salon, doubting if anyone would even notice I'd gone. At this time of evening there was really nothing that needed doing. I went upstairs, thinking I might as well play the radio in my room. I'd sit on the balcony and stare out into the black velvet night. And I ought to write to my sister in Canada; Annabel was overdue a letter. Maybe I'd do that — later on.

As I ambled along the upstairs hall, I could hear faint creaks. Somebody was coming down the uncarpeted attic staircase. I thought nothing of it until, when I opened my bedroom door, the noise stopped abruptly. It was as if the rattle of my latch had given a warning.

Why should one of the servants be so stealthy?

I paused for a moment in the open doorway, listening. But there was only silence. I decided I'd better go along and investigate.

The attic stairs were dark, barely a glimmer reaching up from the landing. I found a switch and a light sprang on at the top. A tall figure stood there, black against the glare.

I recognised instantly who it was. Philip was about half-way up, standing quite still, facing me.

"Perhaps you'd care to explain," I said coldly.

Reluctantly, he started down. He seemed to be moving awkwardly, and when he got closer I could see why. He was carrying something bulky, holding it behind his back.

He gave me a grim smile. "I nearly got away with it, too!"

My eyebrows asked the question.

"Let's not pretend you don't know what I'm talking about," he said scornfully. "Hadn't you better run down and tell the rest of them that you've caught me redhanded?"

I shook my head at him weakly,

bewildered by this suddenly inflammable situation. Absurdly, I began wishing I hadn't decided to come up to my room just now. Then I'd not have heard Philip on the attic stairs; then I wouldn't have been faced with the need to make a decision.

"I haven't the least idea what this is all about," I said, managing to stay icily cold. "But it's pretty plain that you're up to something shady. What's that you're hiding?"

Philip hesitated.

Just in case he imagined I still had any personal interest in what he got up to, I let him have it between the eyes. "As far as I'm concerned I don't give two hoots what your game is. But I happen to work for Miss Harcourt, and I've got a duty towards her."

"I'm sure you have."

From behind his back he produced a painting. It was some twenty inches by fifteen, and seemed to be of a woman's head and shoulders. But I couldn't see it very clearly, and Philip made no attempt to show me.

"Tell me," he asked, "was it chance

that brought you upstairs at that precise moment? Or did you suspect me already?"

"Suspect you of what? That you'd try to steal one of Miss Harcourt's paintings?"

"You know damn well I'm not."

"Then what are you doing with it?"

He was looking at me closely. "You puzzle me," he said slowly. "I just can't fathom you at all."

I was getting mad at this riddle talk. "Look here, if you refuse to explain what you're up to, then I'll have to go down and tell Miss Harcourt."

Again he studied my face, his eyes serious. Then he said heavily: "God knows, I'm probably making a prize idiot of myself, but I'll give you the benefit of the doubt. I'll assume you don't know what's going on at the *Stella d'Oro.*"

"What are you talking about?"

We both turned sharply, hearing the clip-clop of footsteps on the main staircase. Somebody was coming up.

"We don't want to be seen now," Philip whispered urgently. "Come on!"

Catching hold of my wrist fiercely, he dragged me along the landing. He had whipped open the door of his bedroom and thrust me into the darkness before I could protest.

"Hey, you can't just ... !" I began indignantly as the door shut behind us. His hand came clamping over my mouth.

"Be quiet," he hissed.

I could have shaken free, but I let his hand stay across my lips while we both listened. We heard the click of the Blunt's door closing. I guessed Rosalind was another refugee from boredom.

Philip let me go then, and put on the light. "Sorry if I hurt you," he said carelessly, "but I had to stop you giving us away."

I stepped a pace back. "I could have walked out if I'd wanted. You certainly couldn't have stopped me."

His lips curled in a smile of cynical amusement. "And how would you have explained being in my bedroom?"

"I'd have told the truth, of course."

"Ah, but what is the truth, Kerry?"

Did he mean the truth about us — that curious magnetic force that had gripped us? Or was he talking about the strange happenings at the *Villa Stella d'Oro*? I

121

didn't know. I only knew that he had called me Kerry again.

I said nothing, because to have said anything would have given too much away.

Philip was still carrying the picture. He held it up so we could both see.

"What do you think of it?"

The woman was dressed in a medieval style and held a yellow rose clutched to her ivory bosom. The colours were dimmed with age.

"What do you mean — what do I think of it?"

He was looking at me in a sort of puzzled fury, his eyes full of doubt. It was just as though our positions were reversed — as though *he* had caught *me* out in suspicious circumstances.

"It's a simple enough question, isn't it?" he demanded harshly. "What do you think of this painting?"

Vaguely, I looked at the picture again. "I . . . I'm afraid I don't know much about painting . . . "

"Oh come now." He was impatient. "If I were to tell you it's a Raphael would you believe me?"

"Yes, I suppose so." I'd never have guessed for myself, but now that Philip pointed it out . . . I began to get excited. "A Raphael! But that's fantastic!"

Philip crushed me. "I didn't say it was a Raphael."

"But you did, surely . . . ?" I floundered. "Oh . . . I get you — it was painted by one of his pupils?"

Philip switched on the lamp by his writing table, and studied the painting carefully in the better light. He must have taken several minutes, while I watched him, feeling foolish.

At last he said thoughtfully: "I'd say this was painted within the last twelve months, though it's quite a clever piece of work. Very crafty!"

"You mean — it's a deliberate forgery?"

"That's right. Not in the top class, by any means. It's certainly not good enough to fool an expert."

"You being the expert?" I said sarcastically. His superior manner was getting me mad.

He wasn't a bit put out by my sneer. "Without undue modesty, I *am* by way of being an art expert."

Badly shaken, my comeback was too slow to be really effective. "That should make a nice change from selling electric switchgear, or whatever it is you're supposed to do."

"Perhaps we'd better forget that story," Philip said airily.

"Are you telling me now it isn't true?"

He was unrepentant. "You asked me what I did, so I fed you my cover story. I couldn't risk you talking out of turn. After all, I didn't know anything about you."

"And don't want to know, it seems." My voice was sour. "You made that perfectly clear the moment you turned up here."

There was a tiny pause. "How did you expect me to act?" Philip asked coldly. "After putting it out that you'd gone to the United States."

"I wish I knew what you're talking about," I said faintly.

"Do you deny telling your hotel in Rome to say you'd left for the States?"

"Of course I deny it."

Philip said slowly, with false patience: "The receptionist told me distinctly that

124

you and your employer — Monica what's-it? — had quit the hotel; some yarn about her getting married in New York."

"That's perfectly true about Monica getting married. It was all fixed at twenty-four hours' notice. But before going she got me this job with Miss Harcourt."

"Just like that?" scoffed Philip.

"Yes," I snapped. "Just like that."

I knew it must sound nearly incredible to anyone not Monica-hardened. But I didn't see why Philip was entitled to a fuller explanation; I'd been through too much on his account.

"If you had phoned earlier, as arranged," I pointed out, sharply acid, "I would have told you all about it."

"I couldn't phone you earlier. Something cropped up."

And I knew what that something was. Rosalind Blunt had cropped up, and Philip had calmly ditched me for that blonde cutie. He couldn't possible realise I'd spotted him with her on that hotel terrace. Otherwise, he'd never have the nerve to be acting this way.

"I called you as soon as I could," Philip added resentfully.

"The arrangement was that you'd ring in the morning — good and early, you said. I like people who keep their word."

He exploded. "You must have known I'd call later on. How was I to guess a few hours' delay would matter?"

In the ordinary way it wouldn't have mattered. Only a morning of panic, a frozen dread that I'd seen the last of that marvellous man I'd just met. And then he'd have come through, and the world would have zoomed back to bright heaven.

Stabbed through with misery, I twisted the knife. "What was it delayed you, anyway? What cropped up?"

"Business," he said shortly.

"But not electric switchgear business? Some mysterious other business that nobody must know about."

Philip hesitated; then he said reluctantly: "If you must know, I'm acting as buyer for an American art collector."

I too paused, while I digested this. "But why all the secrecy? Why couldn't you have told me in the first place?"

"Don't you see — if the news gets around the prices shoot up at once. I have to operate very cannily."

It made a kind of sense. But I couldn't shake off the feeling of desperate hurt that Philip had lied to me. On a wonderful evening in Rome I'd believed there was complete frankness between us, an open-hearted getting to know one another. If he could have lied about himself so smoothly then, why should I be any more ready to accept this new version?

Maybe *nothing* he said was true. Maybe he just made it all up as he went along, ad-libbing an answer to each of my questions. Would he have admitted anything at all, I wondered, if I'd not threatened to go straight down to Miss Harcourt?

Very well then, I thought angrily, if that's the way it's got to be, then I'll force you to tell me some more. Or invent some more!

"You still haven't told me why you were bringing that painting down from the attic."

"I suspected it was a forgery. But the light up there wasn't good enough to be sure."

"That's all very well, but what right

had you to be up there at all?"

"Every right. If I'm going to be offered the chance to buy an old master, I owe it to . . . to the man I'm working for to make darn sure it's genuine."

"And what makes you imagine you're going to be offered an old master?"

"I know I am." He was going to say something more, but snapped his mouth shut. I waited, and at last he added:

"That's why I was brought here."

"Don't be crazy. Nobody brought you here. You came of your own free will."

"All right then — let's say I was lured here."

"Lured? Who by?"

But Philip wasn't going to be drawn again. "It's a long story. Why don't you trust me, Kerry?"

"Trust *you*? Why should I trust you? Almost everything I know about you is pure fabrication."

He looked hurt. "That's not fair, Kerry."

"You've already admitted you lied to me."

"But I had a good reason for that. I've explained . . . "

"And I don't doubt you'll be just as glib explaining away your other lies — as and when the need arises. I suppose you wouldn't like to swear you're telling me the truth now?"

A deep flush burst upon his face. He fiddled with the picture, turning the canvas over and over in his hands.

"Look here, Kerry, there's no need for you to know the whole story — not yet. Just give me time."

"Time for what? Time for you to steal some of Miss Harcourt's valuable paintings and beat it?"

"You don't really believe that, Kerry."

His eyes burned me with reproach, and I felt myself weakening. He was right, of course. In spite of all the evidence, in spite of knowing him to be a liar, even in spite of catching him redhanded, I couldn't make myself believe he was a thief.

"I know you're up to something, though," I muttered unhappily.

Philip took his time. I could see he was carefully weighing his words.

"Kerry, please just trust me a little. Keep quiet about seeing me with this painting, for a few days at least. Give me a chance to get things sorted out."

"But . . . "

He cut across my protest. "Just a few days, Kerry. What's the harm in that?"

I was all too ready to go along with Philip. It was so much easier than steeling myself to take some positive step against him. Besides, deep down, still not quite dead, was my desire to please him.

Even before I said a word, Philip saw the agreement in my eyes. He knew he had won me over.

Dumping the painting on a chair, he came over to me swiftly. "Thank you, darling . . . "

I was weak enough to let his kiss possess me for a few moments. All my doubts about him fled. I forgot his lies, forgot his deception. I was on the point of responding, of allowing him to know the full extent of his power over me. But just in time the dampening memory of a hotel terrace flashed across my brain.

I thrust Philip away, pushing hard against his chest. "No, don't . . . "

He let me go, just retaining a light hold on my shoulders. "What is it, darling?

What's the matter?"

"I don't want you to do that."

"But I thought . . . "

"Then you thought wrong."

It was only later, back in my own room, that I realised I had never put my consent into words. I'd not promised to say nothing. Philip had sensed my broken resistance, and clinched things with a kiss.

That was all the kiss had amounted to. That was all it had meant to him.

I sat by the open window, staring out into the night. The moon had risen, bathing the stark landscape in cold silver light.

With the sun long gone down, the air was cool on my bare arms. I shivered. But it was some time before I made the effort to go downstairs and join the others.

8

I ALMOST went back on my unvoiced promise to say nothing to Adeline.

When I walked into the salon, there was Philip cosily tucked up beside Rosalind Blunt, the two of them chatting gaily.

For an instant our eyes met and locked. And then the brief contact was over, and he had turned back to the Blunt female.

Adeline rang for coffee. As soon as Carlo wheeled it in, I took charge, glad to have some little job to do.

Inspector Vigorelli decided it was time for him to be going. On his way to the door he paused for a word with me.

"You have quite captivated my young assistant, signorina. He speaks of you all the time. But alas, he regrets that he is so busy as to be unable to call upon you."

Though the Inspector was making a show of speaking confidentially, he hadn't attempted to keep his voice down. I guess he thought any girl would be glad to have flattering remarks overheard.

They'd been overheard all right! A hush was upon the room. I could feel attention riveted on me, tensed for my reply. Even Philip had stopped talking and was staring in my direction.

Inspector Vigorelli was waiting. I had to say something. If I laughed off Cesare's opinion of me as of no consequence, wouldn't that give a victory to Adeline and Zampini? They'd think their protests of the other night had taken effect.

And Philip too — I had an idea he wanted to hear me deny any interest in Cesare.

I handed the inspector a glowing smile. "I enjoyed that drive with him. Cesare is very nice, isn't he?"

"Yes indeed, most pleasant." And then, in a way that made me feel the words were not directed at me at all, he added: "Cesare is a very *clever* young man, signorina."

I retreated to bed as early as I decently could. I felt exhausted and completely bewildered by all the complicated currents and cross-currents of life at the *Villa Stella d'Oro.*

But sleep hung tantalisingly out of reach. My mind skidded uselessly in a bog of contradictory facts, unable to get a grip that would drive me forward.

Overlaying everything else was my extraordinary conversation with Philip. I asked myself again and again if I could believe any single thing he told me.

I'd caught him on the attic stairs with a painting belonging to Adeline. He claimed the thing was a fake, and that he was going to be offered it as genuine. But did that make any sort of sense? It was just plain crazy to suggest Adeline would deliberately sell anyone a forged painting. Hadn't I actually overheard her telling the Blunts that her pictures were only of sentimental value?

That scene in the attic I'd stumbled on still bothered me — I just couldn't make it out. George Blunt, I knew, had made all the running, and pressed Adeline into showing him her paintings. But why had they all of them looked so darned furtive when I'd walked in?

Restlessly, I climbed out of bed and went over to the open window. This time I scarcely noticed the cool night air on my bare arms as I stared out into the silent blackness.

I couldn't forget there was some sort of collusion going on between the Blunts and Zampini. What was it all about? And why had Adeline so flatly refused to believe me when I'd tried to warn her? I was offering her the evidence of my own eyes, and she'd simply brushed it aside.

Of course, I had to admit I was prejudiced against the Blunts — Rosalind, anyway. And against Zampini; it was all too easy to believe the worst of him. I disliked the man. I was revolted by his obscene fatness, and infuriated by his arrogant interference in my affairs.

Adeline was different; I couldn't help being fond of her. Yet though she'd been kind to me in some ways, she'd been quite maddeningly unreasonable in others. And once at least I'd spotted her in a direct lie. I had to remember that Adeline was a superb actress.

My decision not to tell Adeline about Philip's behaviour began to look rather hollow. What would I say? How could I accuse one person of some unspecified wrongdoing to someone who had behaved every bit as suspiciously?

There wasn't a soul at the *Villa Stella d'Oro* I could confide in. Obviously, the sensible plan would be to get the hell out of here; get back to England where life ran on reasonably straight rails.

So why didn't I? Why not go to Adeline the very first thing in the morning and fix it? I needn't have a row with her; just say I wasn't settling down as I'd expected, and wanted to go home.

But 'first thing' stretched to mid-morning, and I had said nothing. Somehow I'd not had the time, what with all the new jobs I'd dug out for myself.

By treading carefully, I'd by now succeeded in getting a minimum of co-operation out of Carlo though he was still prickly as a hollybush. Maria was far more amenable than her nephew. Easygoing, she wanted to get along with everyone, and she always did as I asked quite cheerfully. As for Luciana, her attitude towards me was erratic, influenced by the other two in turn. So I simply praised her whenever possible, and overlooked the small impertinences inspired by Carlo.

Midday came, and still I hadn't tackled Adeline. Over the lunch table I once again allowed her to lead the conversation. Today she declaimed enthusiastically about the season of Greek plays at Syracuse.

"They are superb, Kerry darling. I must take you sometime."

I listened and put in the odd comment when necessary. From somewhere outside of myself, I wondered why I didn't utter the simple words that would have set me free.

And then it was time for Giles to call for me.

He turned up fifteen minutes late, tossing me a careless apology. "Sorry Kerry, but I've got the devil of a rush job on hand right now."

"Well let's skip our date," I suggested. "Make it some other time."

"Not on your sweet life. Now that you've agreed to come, I'm not going to let you dodge it. Let's get moving."

We got moving, zooming down the narrow mountain road like crazy. For want of anything to hang on to, I took a grip on myself.

Giles patted the steering wheel affectionately. "Better than the Sunday runabout that police chap drives, isn't it?" He spoke lightly, but I knew he was getting in a dig about my going out with Cesare.

Tickled, I put on a primness. "I'm not prepared to make invidious comparisons about anything as trivial as a motor car."

"*Trivial*! she says. You women have no soul." Then he had another go. "What about the invidious comparisons you *are* prepared to make — would they be in my favour?"

"I don't know. I like you both."

"Surely not equally?"

I laughed. "Exactly and precisely equally."

The car responded to a sudden surge of power. "Right then, we'll have to sort that out, won't we?"

I'd heard about Taormina before. It certainly was an enchanting place, full of quaint old buildings and fascinating little shops. If I hadn't decided to leave

Sicily I'd want to come again and explore the town properly.

Giles' studio was perched way up the hillside, high above a church. We had to leave the car in a little cobbled square, and climb a steep flight of steps. But the view when we got there was well worth the effort. From his balcony you could look down on the roofs of the old town to the sea far below; or in the other direction away across to Mount Etna.

"It's wonderful, Giles. Aren't you lucky?"

There was just one huge apartment, white-painted throughout with green awnings at the windows to keep off the direct rays of the sun. The room was a tidy clutter, artist's tackle and canvases mixed up with the things of everyday living. The furniture was simple — a small table and chairs, a divan pushed against the wall.

There weren't as many pictures as I'd been expecting. The few Giles showed me were all views of Taormina bay, with only slight variations between them. He was undeniably talented, with an eye for balance and an excellent sense of colour.

But there was a slapdash quality about his work which didn't please me. It suggested a contempt for his tourist customers.

"I'd like to see some of your other paintings, Giles."

"What others?" he asked quickly.

"I mean, the ones you do just to please yourself."

He laughed. "You're certainly a glutton for work, Kerry! I make a living. Why do you imagine I bother to paint anything else?"

"I thought most artists did."

"I doubt it. They all love to talk about the wonderful things they're going to do when they get the time, but it rarely goes further than that."

I noticed there was no canvas on the easel. "What is it you're working on at the moment — the job that's so urgent?"

"Sorry, but I never allow anyone to see anything until I've finished it."

"I can't think why you should be so coy."

He shrugged. "Oh . . . it's a sort of superstition of mine."

More than once as we wandered around

the studio, Giles dropped his arm on to my shoulders. It was an easy gesture that took altogether too much for granted. I twisted away, without making heavy weather of it. But in the end I had to slap him down a bit.

"Giles, please don't!"

"But darling, you can't blame me for taking my chance now I've got you alone at last. You've been holding me off for days."

"Well it's only a matter of days that we've been acquainted."

"Long enough for me to know how I feel about you."

"Oh, don't be silly," I said shakily.

All the same, it was unfair of me to be scornful. I'd hardly taken any time at all myself. Just one short evening with Philip, and I'd been pitched into a sweet helpless turmoil of loving.

But that had been sheer illusion, no more than romantic self-deception. I'd be on stricter guard in future.

Maybe I did like Giles. Maybe I did feel a growing affection for him. But I could no longer trust my surface emotions as a reliable guide.

I needed more time, much more time, to be certain.

Giles was smiling down at me. "All right, darling, I won't rush you." He leaned forward and lightly kissed my forehead.

A sound at the door made us turn quickly. Philip was standing there, staring at us.

"I'm sorry if I'm intruding!" His sarcasm had a sharp edge. "If you remember, Yorke, you told me to drop in when I came down to Taormina."

"Sure thing. Glad to see you." Giles ambled across to him. "Let me offer you something to drink. How about a nice cold beer?"

"Thanks."

While Giles went off to his alcove kitchen, Philip regarded me stonily. "I hadn't realised you were in the habit of visiting Yorke at his studio."

"I've never been here before!" He was forcing me on to the defensive.

"No? Oh well, there always has to be a first time, doesn't there?"

Giles came back, three frosting green bottles clamped in one hand, three tumblers in the other. He poured the beer expertly, sliding it down the glasses.

We stood making polite social noises. Not one of us seemed really at ease.

After a minute or two, Philip began: "I was thinking — I might buy a picture while I'm here. A present for an aunt of mine."

Giles spread his hands in a gesture that swept the studio. "Take your pick."

The men wandered off on a tour of inspection. I sat on the window seat, sipping my lager. I wondered what on earth Philip would make of these facile little paintings, if he really was the expert he claimed to be.

I could hear him passing mildly complimentary remarks.

"You've got a vivid sense of colour, Yorke. And you certainly catch the Sicilian mood."

Giles looked very pleased. "Have I made a sale, then? It'll come in handy for next week's rent."

"Well — they aren't quite what I . . . " Philip paused, frowning. "Have you got anything a bit more . . . traditional, perhaps?"

They moved on to the far end of the studio. As they came back in my direction I heard Giles say: "Make it tomorrow then, Rainsby. About this same time."

"Okay." Philip finished up his beer and put the glass on the table. He looked at me. "I'm heading back to the villa now. Can I give you a lift?"

I didn't fancy being cooped up in a car with Philip, not even for just a quarter of an hour. And anyway, I couldn't go with him.

"Thank you," I said coolly, "but Giles is taking me back."

Philip threw him a questioning look. "It would save you a double trip, Yorke, if Kerry came back with me."

I hadn't a doubt in my mind that Giles would squash this suggestion flat. I was utterly flabbergasted to hear him accepting.

"As a matter of fact, old man, I am rather up to my eyes in it at the moment. It would be a big help if you'd take her."

Shunting me around like an awkward parcel! Philip obliging Giles by taking me home! And Giles being grateful!

I didn't go for this one bit. Jumping up, I said stiffly: "You needn't bother — either of you. I want to have a look round Taormina anyway. I'll grab a taxi later on."

Philip exposed my face-saver. "Won't you want to be back for tea? I know Miss Harcourt likes having everyone around her then."

Weakly, I looked at my watch. Twenty-five past four! "Thanks," I said ungraciously. "Maybe I had better come with you, then." I'd certainly no intention of begging an unwilling Giles to take me back. In fact I'd think twice before accepting another invitation from that one!

He did find the courtesy to mutter an apology as I walked out. "You see, Kerry, I really am terribly busy. I've got to finish that damn thing I'm working on by tomorrow."

On the drive back Philip and I talked in the clipped way of polite strangers thrown together in brief intimacy. For my part I wasn't feeling particularly chatty right then.

"What do you think of Giles Yorke?"

The question was shot at me suddenly.

I gave a grunt and left my opinion wide open.

Philip went on smoothly: "I must apologise if I put my foot in it."

"What are you talking about?"

"I mean, by turning up when I did. But Yorke told me to look in any time, and I naturally didn't expect . . . " He dried up.

"You didn't expect what?"

"Well . . . I had no idea you knew him so . . . "

"Like you, I merely went there to look at his paintings," I cut in hotly.

The story sounded pretty thin, I had to admit. Driving several miles in the blazing heat of afternoon just to see a collection of chocolate-box pictures.

"And what did you think of them?" Philip asked.

"Not much!" Annoyed at being trapped into criticising Giles, I went on to lash out at Philip. "I was surprised you were so interested, considering you're supposed to be such an expert."

Philip was entirely unruffled by the gibe. "I had to be polite, after all. And you must remember, the stuff he has on display is what he sells to the tourists. He'll have something much better tucked away."

"Giles told me he didn't do any other sort of painting."

Philip shrugged. "Most painters get sick of doing commercial potboilers. I expect he has a shot at something better now and then."

"And that's what you're hoping to see tomorrow?"

"Yorke did say he might look something out for me."

But not for me, I thought grimly! For Philip Rainsby, for a prospective buyer, Giles would get out some of his better work. But when *I'd* asked him the same thing it was too much trouble. Just as it was too much trouble to drive me back to the villa.

I scolded myself for minding so much. Why should I care two straws what Giles Yorke did — or what Philip did? I wasn't interested in either of them. They were nothing more to me than casual acquaintances.

The best attitude, I decided, was not to

react to anything more that Philip might have to say. To be neither hostile nor friendly; just plain indifferent.

I thought of some of the nice, uncomplicated men I'd known in London. For the first time I half regretted ever having left my home town.

Philip made several attempts to talk, but in my new mood I let each conversational opening fall flat on its back. I preferred to ponder my own thoughts.

I wondered again why I stayed in Sicily; there was absolutely nothing to keep me. It was true that Adeline had begged me to stay, with fear in her eyes as I'd thought. But Adeline was such a superb actress that I wondered whether any of her emotions were ever genuine.

Yet for all my anger, for all my humiliation at the hands of Philip and Giles, I knew I wasn't going to leave the *Villa Stella d'Oro* — not just yet. Some buried spark of stubbornness made me determined to hang around and see what the mystery was all about.

Back at the villa, I tossed Philip formal thanks for the lift. While he garaged the car I stalked on ahead.

Adeline came hurrying across the hall to meet me. She was in a state of high drama, her silver hair disarrayed, her fists clenched in distress. I could see she had been crying.

This time her emotional display was genuine. This time it was not an act. I knew it.

"Oh Kerry darling! Thank God you are back! I've been almost out of my mind . . . "

"What is it, Miss Harcourt? What's the matter?"

She took a deep, steadying breath and looked at me with eyes that were huge and shadowed. There was real fear in her face, fear in the way she clutched at me.

"Carlo," she whispered hoarsely. "It is Carlo . . . "

"What about Carlo?"

"He is dead!"

"Dead?" I gasped. "But how . . . ?"

"Stabbed to death," she sobbed wildly. "Oh, it is so dreadful, Kerry. What shall I do?"

9

ADELINE leaned on me heavily as I led her through to the salon. Gently, I lowered the old lady into an easy chair, and fetched a glass of brandy.

After a few protesting sips her colour became more normal. But she still lay flopped back in the chair, utterly exhausted.

Zampini was already there in the room, standing over by one of the windows. He watched us in silence for a while. I sensed his impatience.

"Such a fuss!" he burst out. "It is unfortunate, of course. But in Sicily such things must be accepted."

I was appalled. "But this is murder! You can't say murder is normal."

"It is not called murder," he grunted. "A vendetta between two families, a matter of honour. Life is held cheaply here."

"But Carlo had no family," moaned Adeline. "Just his mother and poor Maria,

150

his aunt. That is all . . . "

"It makes no difference. These feuds are carried on to the bitter end."

"Where did it happen?" I asked. "Here at the villa?"

Adeline shuddered. "Oh no, thank God! Not here."

"It was in some back alley at Asiago," muttered Zampini. "It appears he was on his way to visit his mother. It was a custom of his to go every week."

Adeline had heard of Carlo's death by telephone — a call from the police. An hour later they turned up at the villa, two young officers and Inspector Vigorelli himself.

I was rather dismayed that, like Zampini, the police chief seemed to take little account of the killing.

"These things," he said with an indifferent shrug, "they happen."

His men made a brief examination of Carlo's room, and interviewed Maria and Luciana. I doubted if they gleaned any useful information. Both the women were prostrated with grief, weeping noisily and murmuring in constant prayer.

Presumably the inspector had come to

question Adeline and the guests. But he seemed to be treating the occasion rather as another social call. Like any staunch friend at such a time, he nodded his head sympathetically and encouraged Adeline to talk of other things.

It was a tiny incident that brought home how Carlo's death would affect our daily lives. Zampini had gone to pour himself another drink and exclaimed impatiently at finding there were no more bottles of tonic water. He stared at Adeline accusingly. She looked lost.

"Don't worry, Miss Harcourt," I said quickly. "I'll see to it right away."

It would be up to me to see that life went on smoothly at the *Stella d'Oro*. This was a guest house and the guests had to be fed.

Nothing at all had been done in the kitchen. I don't suppose poor Maria had even thought of dinner tonight, and she hardly seemed in any state to cook.

Hoping it was the kindest thing to do, I packed her and Luciana off to their rooms, and started knocking up a simple meal. I was in the middle of grilling lamb cutlets and preparing a huge tomato and cucumber salad, when Cesare Pastore appeared. He came strolling casually into the kitchen.

"You here too?" I greeted him.

"I came to ask you to dine with me," he said calmly, "and then I find all this excitement at the villa."

"Didn't you know about Carlo already?" I asked, surprised. "Your chief is here himself."

"As I discovered. Inspector Vigorelli does not always keep me informed, I'm afraid."

"But you're his assistant."

Cesare shrugged. "Ah well . . . "

I'd not time to talk right then. But when I tried to shoo Cesare out of the kitchen, he offered instead to lend a hand.

"Perhaps I can attend to the grilling of the meat?"

"Well thanks. But don't you Italians regard such things as strictly women's work?"

He grinned at me. "A good policeman must be ready to tackle anything. Between ourselves, I quite enjoy cooking."

I left him guarding the stove while I

laid the tables and fetched wine from the cellar. He kept up a steady flow of chat, calmly picking up where he'd left off each time I dodged back into the kitchen.

"This Carlo . . . Miss Harcourt is upset about him?"

"Yes, she's certainly taking it very hard. I think she must have been quite fond of him." I was recalling the way she had championed Carlo and forbidden me to criticise his work.

"And what did *you* think of him?" Cesare asked.

"Me? Well, he was a good waiter." I spoke with some caution, as I hurriedly made butter curls.

"But you did not like him, I think?"

"I'm afraid I didn't very much. He was rather lazy and could be insolent when he chose."

"Then is it not surprising that Signora Harcourt kept him in her employment?"

"I suppose so. But he was Maria's nephew — perhaps that was why. Poor Maria! And poor Luciana too; they are both dreadfully upset."

"Luciana?"

"She's the housemaid. They were going

154

to be married, I think." I stopped working and looked at Cesare uneasily. "I simply can't understand these vendettas. It all seems so pointless and beastly."

"Who has suggested that this was a vendetta killing?"

"Signor Zampini is sure of it. And your chief seems to have the same idea. It's awful to think they can take it so casually when a man is knifed like that. Do you reckon you'll find the killer?"

"Perhaps. Perhaps not."

Later, while I was setting out the cheese board, he asked: "When did you hear about Carlo's death?"

"After I arrived back from Taormina. Round about a quarter to five."

"Taormina is a beautiful old town, is it not? Did you go down to the bay?"

"No. I only went to Giles Yorke's studio."

"Oh, yes?"

"He had promised to show me some of his paintings."

"I see . . . And then he drove you back here?"

"No. As a matter of fact, I came back

with Philip Rainsby."

Cesare glanced up from the cooking. I don't know why I bothered to explain how the switch had happened, but he seemed interested. I avoided mentioning that I was mad at Giles as a result.

Cesare noticed the omission.

"A man takes a young lady out and does not insist upon driving her home again? Is this how the famous English gentleman behaves?"

Hurt pride made me argue. "But don't you see, Philip was coming back here anyway. It would have been silly . . . "

Cesare regarded me gravely. "The world would be a poorer place if we were not sometimes 'silly'."

He hung around all evening, and I was glad enough to have some help. While I was serving coffee, he even got down to washing the dishes.

"I thought you were supposed to be very busy," I observed when I discovered him with his sleeves rolled up.

"I found I could take a few hours off today. Naturally I came to see you."

"And landed yourself a temporary job as assistant cook and dish washer!"

He stood busily drying plates, smiling into my eyes.

It was past ten before we'd finished. Then Cesare came through to the salon with me. Zampini was there with the Blunts. They told me Adeline had gone to bed. Philip was also upstairs, apparently.

George Blunt buttonholed me at once. "I'd better tell you now, love," he boomed. "Rosie and I will be leaving tomorrow."

"Oh dear!" I was shattered to be losing any of the few guests we had. "Is it because of this business about Carlo? Everything will soon settle down again, you'll see . . . "

He put a heavy hand on my shoulder. "Nothing at all to do with that, love. Just that our plans have changed a bit, that's all. Nowt for you to fret about."

I couldn't really believe him. There had been absolutely no hint of them going, right up to this moment. I tried to persuade him to stay.

"You do understand, Mr. Blunt, all this fuss with the police was not our doing. By tomorrow everything will be back to normal."

Zampini cut across me rudely. "If the

signora and signore wish to leave, that is their affair. You will please not try to detain them."

I had to admire my own restraint in saying nothing to that. But my expression must have said enough. Zampini reddened under his swarthy tan, and muttered a curt apology.

Cesare left soon after eleven, and I made my unhappy way to bed. I'd had plenty and more for one day.

But the day wasn't over after all. I opened my eyes in pitch darkness to a quite unfamiliar sound. I seemed to be hearing it for a long time through a daze of half sleep.

A telephone was ringing somewhere in the villa. I realised it was a sound I'd never heard here before.

I put on the beside light and glanced at my watch. Two-forty-five! Who on earth could be phoning at this hour?

The bell went on and on; a steady, inexorable summons. I slipped into my dressing-gown and hurried downstairs.

At first I couldn't even remember where the phone was. I thought hard as I hustled along. Of course, it was in the lobby near the salon, where I did the flowers.

All this while I expected the ringing to stop. The idea of missing the call worried me for some reason. I had to get there in time.

It seemed ages before I reached the phone and grabbed it up. "*Villa Stella d'Oro.*"

An Italian voice gabbled much too fast for me to pick out even the odd word or two.

"Please, don't talk so quickly ... " I said anxiously. Then a phrase from a tourist handbook leapt into my mind. "*Non parli tanto presto.*"

But the operator had caught and understood my English words. "Signor Zampini is wanted ... A call from New York ... "

"*New York!*" I was astonished. "Did you say New York?"

"Si si. Please, is the signore there?"

10

ZAMPINI was a long time on the telephone. I hung around just out of earshot. Surely something must be dreadfully wrong to bring a transatlantic call in the early hours of the morning?

Much as I disliked the man, I thought I ought to be on hand in case he needed help.

But when Zampini finally emerged, he was white-faced with anger. He brushed past me without a word, without even a glance, storming on up the stairs. I heard a door slam violently.

Bewildered, I switched off the light in the telephone room, closed the door, and made my own way upstairs. I was just going back into my bedroom when I heard voices. Or rather, one voice. It was Zampini, raging at someone in a fury.

I listened anxiously. At first I couldn't make out where the sound was coming from. Not Zampini's own room — that was away down the corridor. Then another voice, feebly protesting, fixed it for me.

"No, Guido. No!"

What an impossible creature Zampini was! To burst in upon an old lady in the middle of the night. And when she was already in a badly shocked state about Carlo. It was sheer heedless cruelty.

I didn't care who he was. I didn't care what he was so angry about. Running down the corridor, I barged straight into Adeline's room without knocking.

The poor old thing was in bed. She had propped herself up on one elbow, blankets clutched to her throat.

Zampini was bending over her. Without straightening, he swung his head towards the door. When he saw me, his face crimsoned into still deeper fury.

"Go away from here!"

"I want to speak to Miss Harcourt." Feeling a lot less calm than I pretended I walked round to the other side of the bed, and sat myself on the edge. Adeline looked up at me tremulously. I put a gentle hand on her shoulder.

"Is there anything I can do?" I asked softly.

Her hand came up and covered mine, pinning it there. The gesture told me how much she needed support. "Perhaps you had better leave us, Kerry."

"I shall stay here as long as you wish it," I said stubbornly. I gave Zampini a challenging stare. "I don't take orders from anyone else."

He sucked in an impatient breath. "Tell the fool of a girl to go away, Adeline."

"You had better do as he says, Kerry." But I knew Adeline didn't mean it. Those thin old fingers were still clutching tight to mine.

When I put my other arm around her shoulders I felt the violence of her trembling. I held her tighter, trying to be reassuring.

"I think *you* had better be the one to go, Signor Zampini," I told him firmly.

"You say that to me?" His fat cheeks shook with anger. "How dare you!"

"My job is to help Miss Harcourt," I said, with a sweet reason he certainly didn't deserve. "Right now she needs rest. I don't know exactly what your position is in this house, but I am asking you to leave the room, if you please."

He looked as if he wanted to pick me up and fling me across the room. Shaken, I still found the courage to stare back at him defiantly.

After a bit he turned away. "Tell her to get out, Adeline," he demanded for a second time.

The terrified old eyes found mine. I knew they were begging me to stay. "You must do as he says, Kerry darling."

"No!" I chose to accept the message of her eyes. "Come now, Signore Zampini. *Please . . . !*"

"You interfering little bitch," he shouted at me. Then he lapsed into a flood of Italian. I waited until he had run out of words before insisting again that he should leave Adeline's room.

"If you refuse I shall go and fetch help."

Fortunately for me, Zampini decided I meant what I said. He went straight to the door.

"I shall see you in the morning," he snarled at Adeline. Then his savage gaze clamped on me. "And you! I shall have something to say to you tomorrow."

But he shut the door with surprising softness.

I tried to be briskly persuasive with Adeline, like a nurse. "Lie down and let me pull the blankets up. You must be cold . . . "

Very meekly, she did what I said. I had an idea she was glad to be taken firmly in hand.

"Now, is there anything I can get you?"

She shook her head. "Nothing, darling. But stay — please stay."

I fetched a chair and sat down close beside the bed. "You mustn't let him upset you so much, Miss Harcourt."

"You do not understand. It is not so simple."

"Why not tell me about it?"

I was cracking with curiosity. I longed to know why that wretched man had so much power over Adeline. Even more, I reckoned it would calm her to confide in somebody.

But she shrank away from the mere thought of telling me. "No, darling, do not ask me. I must not speak . . . "

Should I press her, I wondered, or let

the matter drop? If I was going to protect Adeline from Zampini's wrath tomorrow, I had better know as much as possible before-hand.

The strikingly bold colours of the room were sombre now in the shaded light of a bedside lamp. I glanced around, lost for a moment in my thoughts. The pictures on the walls jolted me back to my talk with Philip. They provided the inspiration I needed.

I plunged straight in. "Is the trouble something to do with forged paintings?"

She reacted so violently that I knew I'd hit the target dead on centre. She gave a little sob and her hands flew to her face.

"I suppose Giles told you? The idiot."

"Giles?" I exclaimed in dismay. "Is he tied up in this, too?"

She looked bewildered. "Then he didn't . . . ?"

"It was just a stab in the dark, Miss Harcourt."

Adeline chewed that over. "I see," she said eventually. "When you saw me with the Blunts up in the attic, you put two and two together?"

I didn't disabuse her. There was no need to drag Philip into this. Not for the moment.

I had a feeling that after the first shock, Adeline was glad I knew. Her fear seemed to have lifted a little. She shook an arm free from under the blankets, and clutched again for the comfort of my hand.

"You must believe me, Kerry darling, there is nothing really wicked . . . What we are doing, it is wrong, yes. But . . . "

I tried to soothe her down. Judgements could come later, if need be.

"It all began as a joke," she went on earnestly. "Not to make money; not with the idea of cheating people. I myself have never profited from it. My share I have always given to the nuns."

"Let's get this straight. You've been selling forgeries as genuine old paintings . . . ?"

She was denying it hotly. "Never! Not once have I made such a claim. But if I sold a nice painting, and the buyer paid much more than he would have done simply because he thought he had found a Raphael, well . . . "

A spark of humour flickered back into her eyes. "The price we got was not a tenth the value of a genuine Raphael — not a twentieth! So who was cheating whom, darling? Tell me that."

I had to know the worst. "Who painted the forgeries, Miss Harcourt? Was it Giles?"

"Yes, it was Giles."

"But why? Why did he have to get himself mixed up in anything like this?"

Adeline rushed to his defence, her affection plain. "The poor boy found it so hard to make a living selling those little paintings to tourists. They will not pay very much for a souvenir. Then one day a couple of years back he showed me something he had done for his own pleasure. It was a portrait of a young woman, very much in the style of Raphael. Guido was staying here at the time, and it was he who thought up the whole scheme. He said it would be amusing to hide the picture in the attics amongst some old paintings I had up there, and persuade somebody to buy it believing they were getting an old master at a bargain price. And it worked without any difficulty."

"The way you've been talking," I said shortly, "it sounds like a regular business."

She smiled faintly, "I'm afraid so. Guido has been sending people over here, ready primed with a story about a silly old woman who doesn't realise she's got a Raphael amongst the lumber in her attic. He would explain that because I know he's an expert, I would smell a rat if he tried to buy it for himself. But for a consideration he will give them my address, to try their luck. The poor fools always fall for it."

The answers to other puzzles were beginning to click into place. I could see now why there were so few visitors to this attractive guest house.

I said rather bitterly: "I suppose the only people you ever have staying here are prospective suckers?"

"No, no, darling!" Adeline was shocked. "That would be much too suspicious. We always have a sprinkling of ordinary guests. Our little honeymooners, for example."

So it boiled down to this — a sordid

confidence trick! The mugs were cleverly blinded to an obvious fraud by their own monstrous greed. They all imagined they were putting one across a simple old lady, whereas in fact a very astute woman was outwitting them.

It was right up Adeline Harcourt's street! A glorious charade, an elaborate performance to bedazzle the poor dupes Zampini prodded to her door. How she must have enjoyed stringing them along, first pretending reluctance, at last being persuaded . . .

And all of it neatly justified in Adeline's mind by giving the profits of crime to a convent. The nuns would be distressed to know the true source of those freewill offerings!

I had thought Adeline had dozed off, but when I shifted in my chair her eyes flashed open. There was more to tell, and having got started she was determined to tell it.

Giles, I learned, had been keeping up a steady trickle of the forgeries, always in the style of the same painter. He had the knack of Raphael, she explained artlessly. Afterwards, when the deal was done, Zampini would be at hand to warn the buyers that the painting must be smuggled out of Sicily. He would tell them they'd never get official permission to remove such a fine work of art.

"We could not risk an intelligent Customs man asking awkward questions," Adeline pointed out.

The answer, it emerged, was simple. Giles would obliterate the 'masterpiece' with a scene of Taormina bay. Hey presto! It had become just another of Giles Yorke's souvenir pictures, well known to the Customs. Who would ever guess what lay concealed underneath?

To me it all sounded highly complicated. And I couldn't see where it got them.

Adeline made an impatient cluck. "For the overpainting, Giles used materials that can easily be removed; and Guido furnished the buyers with an address in their own country where the work can be done. He has contacts everywhere."

"And has nobody ever brought charges against you, when they eventually discover the fraud?"

Her lips curled into scorn at my innocence. "A man will not easily admit to the world that he has been hood-winked. And of course there is nothing criminal in what we do. I have never so much as hinted that a painting might be genuine."

"You didn't need to. Zampini had already done that job for you."

Reluctantly she admitted it. "I have been wanting to stop for some time. But it is so difficult. What started as a mere amusement has got out of hand."

"How can you call it amusement?" I asked reproachfully. "It's downright dishonest, whatever you say."

There was a silence before she answered slowly: "You are right, of course, Kerry darling. I should never have started this silly game."

Even now, I doubted if Adeline could really understand the wrong in what she'd been doing. Her need to *perform* was so strong-rooted; it justified almost anything.

I said firmly: "Tomorrow you must tell the Blunts it was all a mistake. And then finish with the whole wretched business."

Despite her obvious guilt, Adeline had

been telling the story with a sort of inner amusement. She was still half-enjoying the joke. But my suggestion stunned her. She looked really frightened then.

"But Guido would never agree to that."

"So what?" I asked impatiently. "Just tell him you're not prepared to carry on any longer."

In a snap she became a feeble old lady once more. Her words jerked out in little sobs. "I cannot do that . . . You don't know him . . . !"

"There's nothing he can do about it. He can't *force* you."

"I dare not!" she cried. "I dare not tell him . . . "

"Then I will."

"No!" She yelped the word in startled terror. "You must not say anything, Kerry. It is too dangerous. You must not allow Guido to know I have told you so much."

"I don't see why not. If he knows that I know, he won't risk carrying on."

She had lifted her head from the pillow, shaking it wildly from side to side, refusing to listen to me.

"Why are you so afraid of Zampini?"

I asked, puzzled. "It's as if he's got some kind of hold over you."

"Oh, you do not understand," she moaned. "He is my friend. He was poor dear Vittorio's friend too."

"A funny sort of friend to have! Terrifying the life out of you."

Very quietly Adeline whispered: "In Sicily, it is like that."

"What do you mean?"

"The villa is isolated, you see." She spoke as if this accounted for everything. But I didn't catch on.

"We need protection," she explained. "We must have a friend in the . . . the Old Movement."

It took a second to click. "The Mafia, you mean?"

Nervously, she skated away from the word. "Guido was Vittorio's contact. His friend. After Vittorio's death, when I inherited the villa, Guido became *my* friend."

I was appalled. "But you treat him like a real friend."

"It is something one learns to accept."

"And if you refuse to accept it?"

She put up her hands to her cheeks.

"I am so afraid of Guido. He will stop at nothing . . . " She hesitated, and then added quietly under her breath: "Look what happened to Carlo."

The fear I'd been contemptuously dismissing got a sudden swift stranglehold. I shivered, beginning to understand why Adeline was so afraid. The squalid traffic in forged paintings had all at once become charged with sinister overtones.

"What do you mean about Carlo?" I faltered.

Huge tears trembled upon the old lady's eyelids. They slid slowly down her cheeks and wet the white pillows with dark rings.

There was a long, heavy silence.

"I should never have told you so much," she murmured sadly at last. "It was unfair of me."

"What did you mean about Carlo?" I persisted. "The police said it was because of a vendetta, a family rivalry."

Adeline was worn out. Her whispered words came very slowly. "Carlo also knew too much, and he was blackmailing me . . . "

"*Blackmailing* you?" I grated out.

"I did not really mind that — it was only a little money. But Guido was furious when he found out this morning."

"Are you really saying ... ?" I hesitated at the very brink. The idea was too fantastic. Adeline must have meant something quite different.

Seconds added together until they seemed like whole minutes before she summoned the energy to speak again.

"Yes, it was Guido. I do not know who did the actual knifing, but Guido was responsible for Carlo's death. I am certain of it."

11

I STAYED the rest of the night in Adeline's bedroom. I had to. I dared not leave her alone with Zampini possibly still on the prowl.

Unfortunately, I had chosen a high-backed chair with hard nobbles which prodded my spine. By the time they were getting painful it was too late to do anything. Adeline was asleep, her fingers locked tight into mine.

Her slowly hissing breath punctuated heavy silence. The rhythm was hypnotic. My mind drifted, building a weird picture montage of the story she'd just told me. A walking nightmare. Overshadowing everything else was the climax of horror. A handsome young Sicilian being violently done to death!

I could see every sharp detail of that back alley drama, except for the murderer himself. He was a shapeless black blur in my mind. Had Zampini's own hand held the knife? Or was it wielded by some cheaply-bought assassin?

I didn't doubt the truth of what Adeline had told me. So much was explained now; so much had clicked into place — neatly, nastily, horribly. The elaborate plot and counter-plot, the double bluff. And all acted out with superb professional skill against the beautiful backcloth of the *Villa Stella d'Oro.*

To Adeline it had been just a game, a harmless enough joke. And while she was laughing, Zampini counted his profits, ruthlessly exterminating an upstart waiter who had tried to get in on the act.

What about Giles? I brooded sadly. Just how deeply was he involved?

I understood now why he'd so eagerly abandoned me to Philip yesterday afternoon. He'd had a rush job on hand, going hell for leather covering George Blunt's fake Raphael with a stock view of the bay. Once a deal was done, they'd want to get rid of the sucker, and fast.

To my surprise I found I wasn't all that cut up about Giles. I'd been kidding myself about him, I realised — trying to *make* myself fall for him. But all along I'd known I couldn't really do it. Never in a hundred years. Not while Philip Rainsby was on the same planet.

Yet I'd raised a tight guard against Philip; wanting to trust him, but not daring to. If only I could believe his every word, uncritically, without reservation. But I was faced with his own admission that he'd lied to me.

I still couldn't decide if even now he was being honest with me. Why should a professional art buyer hang around at the *Stella d'Oro* if he expected to be offered forgeries? Was it because he was so infatuated with Rosaline Blunt?

The more I knew, the more I didn't know. Philip, Giles, Adeline, Carlo. And Zampini . . .

Why had the vicious Italian been in such a tearing rage, ranting at Adeline in the middle of the night? She'd told me a lot, but she hadn't explained that.

Unburdened, the old lady looked very peaceful. Now that her fear of Zampini was shared with me, she was able to let go and lose herself in sleep.

I wished I could do the same.

Sitting here beside her, my mind adrift, was sheer escapism. I was sidestepping the problem of what I was going to do in the morning.

I needed advice. I needed help. And there was only one person I could conceivably go to. I'd got to trust Philip. I had to assume, whatever his game might be, that in the final analysis he was on the right side.

My watch pointed the improbable fact that it was already half past six. I couldn't delay any longer.

Adeline still slept. Stiff from my long vigil, I got up without disturbing her. I opened the bedroom door and put a cautious ear into the corridor.

Silence! Everything was utterly quiet. Even the servants were not about yet.

I hated leaving Adeline. Zampini might come back while I was gone, to have another go at her.

I decided to lock her in. He'd hardly be likely to have a key to the door. And if he was mad enough to force it open, I'd be sure to hear him. Swiftly I shifted the key from inside to outside, and turned it.

Early sun blazed the length of the corridor. After the gloom of Adeline's bedroom I was half blinded. Blinking,

I made my way to Philip's door, and tapped gently.

There was no reply.

I tapped again, rapping with my knuckles this time. I was afraid of making too much noise. Zampini's room was not very far away.

At length I tried the handle. It turned, and I opened the door a few inches.

"Philip!" I called softly. "Are you awake?"

There was still no answer.

The bedroom was dark, the thick curtains drawn across. I slipped inside, shutting the door behind me before snapping on the light switch.

Philip was not there! The bed was rumpled, but empty.

My bitter disappointment told me just how much I'd been depending upon Philip. I knew now that I'd been banking on him to sort out the mess. I'd wanted him to decide what to do.

Had he just happened to get up early to go walking while it was fresh? Checking, I felt the bed sheets. They were cold, quite cold.

Philip had been gone for some time.

What was he up to, out of his room at the crack of dawn?

At a loss, I went outside again. There was still no sound, no stirring of life in the big house.

I'd left Adeline locked in, so she would be safe enough while I investigated downstairs.

But Philip was nowhere around. Not in the salon or the dining-room. Nor, as far as I could see through the windows, was he outside on the loggia, or anywhere in the gardens.

Half-heartedly, I tried the kitchen regions. And then, on a sudden thought, I went round the back of the house to the old stables where his hired car was garaged.

It was gone.

The big Mercedes that Zampini used was also missing.

It was while I was dressing, miserably wondering what to do next, that I heard a car draw up outside. Just the faint scrunch of tyres as it braked.

Hastily I stepped into my dress and zipped it up. Giving my hair the merest flick of a comb, I ran out to see who had turned up.

Philip was just reaching the head of the staircase. For an instant he looked plain startled to see me. Then a masking smile fell upon his face.

"Hallo, Kerry . . . "

While he walked up to me, I waited in silence, held back by newly surging doubts. But again it came to me — who else dared I trust?

Cesare? But turning to Cesare for help would mean bringing him in officially, as a policeman. I couldn't ask him not to report what I told him.

Was it fair, at this stage, to fetch the weight of law down on Adeline's head? The old lady had got herself involved much deeper than she had ever intended, driven by Zampini into perpetrating more and more frauds. She wasn't really a criminal. The whole of life was a stage play to Adeline Harcourt, every action studied, every emotion over-expressed. She had gone into this forgery business as nothing more than a piece of light comedy. She had meant no harm beyond burnt fingers for a few greedy amateur art collectors who could no doubt well afford the loss, anyway.

And I believed what she'd told me about her share of the profits going to the nuns of Santa Teresa. I could imagine that to Adeline this would seem to be squaring the account, a sort of moral tit-for-tat.

No, I couldn't speak to Cesare; not until I knew more than I did now.

I realised that Philip was waiting for me to say something. I thought he looked a bit ill-at-ease, as though he'd been hoping to slip into his room unnoticed. But I couldn't be sure of that. The low-slanting sun was shining straight into my eyes, and his face was half in shadow.

"What is it, Kerry?" he said at last.

Was I to confide in him, or not? Should I boldly take a chance and ask for Philip's help, or timidly hold back and risk an even worse outcome?

There could only be one answer.

"Please, I want to talk to you. It's important." I threw open the door of my room again, and walked in. He followed me, slowly. I could tell he was very unwilling.

The moment the door was shut, I

challenged him directly. "Where have you been?"

His silent stare asked me what business that was of mine.

"I mean," I added weakly, "going off so early in the morning . . . "

He took his time about replying. His lips curled in a faint, unamused smile. "I just went out."

He wasn't going to tell me, and I couldn't make him.

"What was it you wanted to say to me, Kerry?"

Doubt made a last-ditch stand. To overcome my reluctance to talk, I had to rush in. I flung the story at his head so wildly it must have been almost incoherent.

"Those forged paintings . . . you were right about them. Zampini's the one . . . and Giles too — he does the actual work. And Adeline Harcourt's in it as well . . . "

He listened impatiently as though I were talking gibberish. I had expected him to congratulate me, but the moment I took a pause for breath, he slid a damper in.

"You've got it all wrong, Kerry. You're imagining things."

I was staggered. "But it was you . . . What about that painting you showed me?"

He was frowning. "I suppose I am to blame. I shouldn't have put fool ideas into your head."

"Ideas!" I blazed at him. "Are you saying now the picture was *not* a fake?"

He looked like a man caught on the hop. "You see, Kerry, a thing is only a fake if it pretends to be something else. A painting might be very like a Raphael, but if nobody tries to make out it's genuine, then it can't possibly be called a forgery."

"But you told me it was going to be offered to you as a genuine Raphael."

"It seems I was mistaken. Nobody's made any approach to me up to now."

This is crazy! I was beginning to wonder if I'd been dreaming last night.

I tried hard to stay calm. "Don't you understand? Adeline Harcourt actually confessed to me. She explained the whole set-up."

Philip had turned away. He was fiddling

185

with my hairbrush as if its exact position on the dressing table was important.

"Maybe the poor old girl's getting a bit senile," he suggested. "I've half suspected it before."

"That's absurd, and you know it," I flared angrily. "She's perfectly sane."

Still with his back to me, he shrugged indifferently. "Well then, I can only suggest you misunderstood what she was saying."

I couldn't get through to Philip at all. He wasn't just a stranger; he was more like an enemy.

I had to screw down my safety valve hard. In my indignation I'd have stalked out then and there, but I couldn't very well leave him in my bedroom. Instead, I flung open the door and pointedly stood beside it.

"If you choose to believe I've imagined the whole thing, then you'd better just forget what I've said."

He came across to me quickly, and pushed me aside so he could shut the door again. "That's what you must do too, Kerry — forget it. Put it right out of your mind."

I managed to look him straight in the eye. "Is that meant to be an order?"

As I'd intended, he was quite put out. "It's just . . . well, you can't go around accusing people . . . "

"But it's perfectly all right when the accusations are made by Philip Rainsby, I suppose?"

"I only told you what I believed was true at the time."

"That's exactly what I'm doing, isn't it? And I've got a lot more to go on than you had."

He didn't try to answer that one. Neither did he make any move to go. He stood with his back to the door, as if waiting for me to cool down.

It was no wonder I was at boiling point. I'd been banking on Philip's help in coping with something too big to handle alone. And he'd failed me!

I wanted to flop down on my bed in despair.

If only I could somehow go to the police without implicating Adeline — and Giles, too. If only I could somehow pin it on Zampini alone; he was the real villain.

I longed to be able to share my problem with Philip. But he stubbornly refused to admit there was any problem at all.

He'd have to admit it if I told him what Adeline suspected about Carlo's death — that Zampini had been behind it. He'd have to believe me then. Surely he couldn't brush me off any longer?

But some deep-buried caution held me back, I looked right into Philip's eyes, wondering again if I dared trust him that far. All my doubts about him were flickering to life once more.

I'd have to be getting back to Adeline's room. Maybe talking to her again might give me an idea. Maybe she herself would be willing to act decisively this morning.

Philip was still standing there, his back square to the door.

"Please!" I said curtly. "You're in my way."

He shrugged and stepped to one side. I opened the door and stalked straight out.

"Kerry!" he called after me. "Please don't do anything silly."

I didn't answer. I didn't even look back

as I walked briskly away.

The key was clutched ready in my hand. As I jabbed it home I felt a slight resistance, and there was a soft thud on the bedroom carpet.

I didn't have to turn the key; the door had already been unlocked from the inside.

In a flurry of panic I burst into Adeline's room. The bed was empty. She was gone. I checked her bathroom and she was not there either.

12

I HUSTLED downstairs and for the second time that morning did a quick tour of the ground floor rooms. Now I was searching for Adeline.

I'd locked her in. Obviously she must have had a duplicate key and let herself out. But after the terror I'd seen in the old lady last night, I had to find her quickly and reassure myself that she was safe.

To my astonishment I found her tranquilly discussing the luncheon menu with Maria. The cook, still tearful, was clearly back on duty and ready for work. Luciana, also puffy about the eyes, was hovering in the background.

Adeline swung round on me, alert and smiling. "Ah, there you are, Kerry darling. We might as well have breakfast right away, then."

She could smile at a time like this! She could even think of eating!

"But I ... Look here, we've got to talk ... "

"Yes darling, what is it?" The question was tossed at me casually. She turned away to speak to Luciana, and my Italian just coped with a rough translation: the girl was being told to take our breakfast out to the loggia where it would be cooler.

Adeline's behaviour this morning was uncannily calm. It was as if last night's drama had never happened.

And that, I discovered, was her story. Or very nearly.

"Did I really say those things, darling?" Her laugh tinkled merrily. "I must have been dreaming. Actually, I *was* just a wee bit naughty. I had an extra cognac before I went to bed."

I simply couldn't believe my ears. I said stonily: "You were perfectly sober, Miss Harcourt. You were also perfectly lucid."

"How amusing . . . !" She might have been playing a dowager duchess on the West End stage. "If I was really as sober as you say, darling, then I can only suggest that perhaps you are . . . imagining a little?"

"I am not imagining anything. You

must surely remember what you told me as well as I do. What about Signor Zampini and Carlo?"

Her eyes first narrowed, and then opened wide in a beautifully contrived expression of bewilderment. "What about Guido and poor Carlo?"

I barely more than whispered it. "You said that he had Carlo ... done to death."

Adeline reacted in the character she'd chosen. Angry astonishment was rigidly contained within a superb dignity. "My dear girl, how can you put such dreadful words into my mouth?" But slowly her expression of shocked, tight disapproval dissolved into a roguish smile. "But of course! You are joking, darling. And I fell into your trap."

I insisted that I most certainly was not joking, but she simply would not listen. When a moment later Zampini appeared on the loggia, she beckoned him over.

"Guido, our young friend has been teasing me." To my amazement she went on: "Kerry is pretending that last night I told her a perfectly crazy story about you and I plotting to sell forged paintings to my guests. She even makes out that I confessed to being terrified of you. Think of it, my dear Guido!"

I expected an outburst of fury, but a muted response from this man was even more frightening. He wagged a finger at me, a fat, playful finger.

"You British and your practical joking! Will you never stop?"

What could I say? That I had not been kidding? That I believed everything Adeline had told me, however much she might deny it now?

While I still gaped at him, too startled to utter a word, he turned and stumped off. The grotesque body was trembling with laughter. He eased himself down at a table on the far side of the loggia, and shook out a large white napkin.

Three minutes later Philip came out to join Zampini, giving Adeline a charming smile as he passed. I got no more than a curt nod.

All through breakfast Adeline ate placidly. Each crusty morsel of her roll was thickly dabbed with butter and red cherry jam. She appeared to be completely unperturbed, merely giving me an occasional pursed-lips smile of amused reproof when she caught my eye.

Most of the time I was watching the two men at the other table. Luciana had brought them a basket of rolls and a large pot of coffee. They both tucked in heartily, and seemed to be talking together with real gusto — more friendly than I'd ever seen them before.

Adeline began a desultory conversation. Or rather a monologue, because I contributed next to nothing. From time to time she tried to coax me to eat, pretending to imagine I was refraining through some foolish idea of dieting.

"You modern girls — all you think about is your figure. Now in my day it was fashionable for a woman to have a bit more flesh on her bones ... "

Her voice, running steadily on, made no impact upon my mind. I cut right across her. "I shall have to tell the Blunts — you realise that?"

Adeline didn't attempt to finish what she'd been saying. There was a short enquiring pause, then: "You will tell the Blunts what, darling?"

"That the painting they bought from

you is a forgery. Or do you now deny you sold them a painting at all?"

She gave me a little puzzled frown. "George certainly *wanted* to buy one of my nice pictures. But of course I couldn't possibly let anything go. It would have been unfair to ... to Vittorio's memory."

The crazy mixed-up atmosphere of the villa made me suddenly vicious. I swooped in with a savage dig.

"Vittorio? Or do you mean unfair to the memory of your Italian ancestor who built this villa two hundred years ago?"

At least I'd managed to startle her for a moment. But then she was smiling serenely again. "So you overheard that little tale, did you? But darling, you cannot blame me if sometimes I stir in a little romance and colour for the benefit of my guests. It pleases them, you see. And it is quite harmless."

"Harmless fiction can sometimes prove quite dangerous before it's done with," I pointed out coldly.

Her look reproached me for the unpleasing thought.

The sun was slowly mounting higher.

Already the heat outside would be fierce, but sheltered by hanging greenery the loggia stayed pleasantly fresh.

The scene was restful normality — comfortable people at ease in delightful surroundings, taking a leisurely breakfast as a prelude to a day of happy relaxation.

In undertones, the men joked. Adeline sipped her coffee. She had composed herself into a picture of elegance and charm, an elderly lady without a care in the world. I had to make myself remember that she was a consummate actress.

Despite the coolness of the shade-splashed loggia, I was sweating. My skin boiled. My tight-stretched nerves were being screwed mercilessly to screaming point.

Adeline was regarding me steadily. Her eyes held a secret challenge.

"I believe that Giles sold George Blunt one of his little harbour scenes. The tourists always fall for them. Of course, one must admit they are very colourful in their simple way . . . "

"This is absurd!" I stood up swiftly, scraping my chair on the flagstones. "I am going up to the Blunts right now and have it out with them. They've got to be protected from themselves."

Quite deliberately I had been speaking loud enough for my words to carry to Philip and Zampini. But both of them pretended not to hear.

Adeline popped a last bite of roll into her mouth before observing mildly: "George and Rosalind Blunt have left already, darling."

"*Already!* But how?"

"Guido drove them down to Taormina first thing. I expect they got a cab from there to the airport at Catania."

So the Blunts had been hustled out of the villa at daybreak — obviously to get them out of my way. Zampini had worked fast. I wondered what story he'd spun to convince them they must leave Sicily without delay.

"I . . . I could probably still reach them by telephone," I said uncertainly.

"I cannot imagine why you should want to contact them, darling. Anyway . . . " Adeline consulted her watch, "they will be airborne by now, I'm afraid."

I dropped back into my chair, defeat

weighing me down. I didn't doubt that all other evidence was carefully removed by now. If there had ever been any other evidence!

Whoever would accept a few paintings resembling Raphael's work, found lying in the attic of the *Stella d'Oro* or in Giles Yorke's studio, as constituting proof that a conversation I'd happened to overhear, in which Adeline had shown absolutely no interest in selling any of her pictures, was all part of a cunningly planned deception?

Still, if I made them stop the racket here and now, wouldn't that be good enough? Even though I couldn't actually prove anything, they'd hardly dare carry on once I'd threatened to expose them.

In any case, I guessed there was little enough I could do about the pictures already sold. And even supposing I did succeed in making a public issue of the swindle, would past buyers like George Blunt thank me for it? Would they want their names dragged through the courts? Would they relish the world knowing they'd been fooled by a simple confidence trick?

It was just this built-in reluctance of the dupes to come forward that made the swindle so darned clever. Every single one of those ready-and-willing customers had deserved to get his fingers burned. Every one had been motivated by sheer greed.

It was an easy solution just to let it go. But I'd warn Adeline that they must stop at once. I'd face up to Zampini and threaten him with exposure if he didn't promise an end of this wretched business.

And Philip — exactly where did he stand in the scheme of things? Was he working with the others in some subtle way? Was the story he'd told me about being a buyer for an American art collector as much a lie as his earlier yarn that he was employed by an electric switchgear firm?

Seeing him now, so friendly with Zampini, how could I possible believe anything else?

It was crazy for me to stay here any longer. I'd have to leave the *Villa Stella d'Oro*; leave Sicily; leave Italy. I'd have to go back to London and try to put this whole unhappy episode out of my mind.

My trip to Italy had started so excitingly. At first it had been such fun with Monica in Rome. But now it was ending in disaster. To go home and forget was the only sensible thing to do.

Bit by bit I was lulling myself into taking the easy course. I was kidding myself along with false reasoning. I was playing a con trick on myself.

But I saw through it. How could I keep quiet about what I knew? How could I go away as long as Carlo's death was still not fully explained? Adeline had definitely accused Zampini. She pretended now that she had never said so, but I wasn't imagining a single thing about that conversation in the night.

I ought to remain here, waiting and watching. I ought to hang on at the *Stella d'Oro* until one or other of the swindlers slipped up; until I got some tangible evidence about Carlo's death.

Yet against this strong argument, I wondered if it wouldn't be foolish to stay on. The police were apparently quite satisfied that Carlo's death had been a vengeance killing. Surely they ought to know? They understood local attitudes and Sicilian morality far better than I did.

So far I hadn't eaten a thing for breakfast. That wouldn't do at all. If I were serious about giving the gang a false sense of security, I'd have to behave normally.

I reached out and took a roll from the delicate wicker basket. Carefully, I buttered a fragment and put it in my mouth. It was like chewing dry chaff.

Adeline watched with approval. "There's a sensible girl, Kerry." Did she mean for eating something? Or did she mean for bowing to the inevitable?

As I took a mouthful of coffee to wash down the bread, I caught Adeline's nod towards the two men. Even her smallest movements were always distinct and very expressive. What I read into this little gesture was satisfaction that things were under control.

She was telling Zampini that I wasn't going to argue; that I was accepting the situation.

I wondered if Philip was included in that message.

13

IT became hotter than ever as the morning dragged on. Life at the *Villa Stella d'Oro* dissolved into a fantastic dream sequence.

Zampini's behaviour had changed dramatically. Now he was full of wreathing smiles that cracked his face. He even tried to flirt with me, using a quaintly formal raillery.

Philip hung around all the time. He observed Zampini's extraordinary antics without seeming in the least put out. I wondered bitterly why I even thought he should have been.

I went through my routine jobs with a mechanical lack of interest. The villa was usually cool indoors but today it felt stiflingly oppressive. The kitchen was unbearable, the big oven adding fiercely to the stunning heat. Red-eyed, Maria and Luciana carried on with a forlorn resignation that was unutterably sad. I wished there was some comfort I could offer them.

The flowers had to be done each day and that promised to be a happier job. But when I went outside the sun savaged me, its searing brilliance climbing right into my eyes.

Pietro was nowhere around. I discovered him eventually stretched out asleep under a tree at the end of the cypress walk. It was so unusual to find the old man slacking that I hadn't the heart to waken him. Anyway, did I care any longer about the *Stella d'Oro*? The flowers could wait.

I was close by the garden pavilion, fluted columns arching to a white dome. Its soft pool of shadow tempted me inside.

I had scarcely sat down when I heard a scrape of feet on the steps. Guido Zampini was following me in.

Panic took hold of me, a sudden terror of being alone with this man. But then I remembered that old Pietro was dozing within earshot. He was bound to hear if I cared to yell out. And anyway, we were barely fifty yards from the villa itself.

I steeled myself to face Zampini with a show of calm. He came waddling across the blue mosaic floor, his face smiling, his eyes flinty. "I see you have discovered the best place, my dear Signorina Lyndon. Even though I am accustomed to heat, I find this too much." With a sigh he flopped down beside me on the marble seat.

I edged away. Zampini had always revolted me, but now I felt a paralysing fear which reason couldn't dismiss. Last night Adeline had nailed him as the man behind a brutal killing. Her subsequent denials hadn't budged my belief that she was probably right. He looked the type. He looked capable of every kind of evil.

I sat there smiling at him feebly, wondering how soon I could make my escape. Then his muttered exclamation of disgust made me turn round to see Philip standing at the entrance.

"Good morning, again, Miss Lyndon."

He began speaking to Zampini in Italian that was far too fluent for me to follow. I got the impression he was asking for help or advice. Zampini's genial smile tightened noticeably, the effort behind it showing.

After his formally polite greeting, Philip

hadn't looked at me once.

At last Zampini lumbered to his feet with obvious reluctance. "My regrets, signorina, but this young man asks me to look at his automobile. He cannot make the engine work." The Italian threw his hands upwards, expressing helplessness. "It is of no avail that I tell him I know little about mechanical matters. He should telephone the garage from which he hired the machine . . . " He backed away, bowing.

Philip flickered his eyes towards me, but before I could read their expression he was taking Zampini's arm in the matiest way, spouting some more unintelligible Italian.

They went off together and I was left alone. What was I to make of Philip's sudden appearance? I couldn't believe that he genuinely needed Zampini's assistance with his car. Had that been merely a blind — and excuse to talk urgently with his confederate? Or could it have been for my benefit? To save me from Zampini's nauseating pleasantries?

I had no means of knowing. Listlessly I got up and wandered back to the villa, quite forgetting the flowers I had come out to collect.

I drifted through the rest of the morning. Between us Luciana and I had to do Carlo's work, but with so few guests left it didn't amount to much. I laid the tables for lunch, and afterwards carried a bucket of ice into the salon in case anybody wanted drinks. Philip was in there, reading. He barely glanced up at me.

As I went across the hall, Zampini was coming out of the telephone room. I thought again of that mysterious phone call from New York which had sparked off his sudden raging outburst in the night. And yet, looking around the place now, a stranger might well have imagined that everything at the *Villa Stella d'Oro* was peacefully normal.

And so it was perhaps. As peacefully normal as a doomed town on the countdown to an earthquake. As peacefully normal as Mount Etna, smoking wispily under the rearing Sicilian sun. And like Etna, the *Stella d'Oro* might storm into eruption at any moment. Violence had already touched the lives of those living here. Next time it might strike right inside the villa itself.

Was I being a fool not to clear out now?

About noon Giles came wandering in. He grabbed me cheerily, but underneath he was in a queer mood. He seemed to be treading warily, like he wasn't too sure of himself.

It hit me that maybe he was here under orders. Zampini had used the phone this morning. Was it to instruct Giles to come to the villa and butter up this nuisance of a girl who knew too much?

I decided to challenge him straight out.

Cunningly I worked it so that Giles and I were alone on the loggia. But before I got a chance to speak, Zampini came bouncing out, full of his new hard-sweating palliness. And Philip followed close on Zampini's heels. From then on I didn't get a single minute alone with Giles.

I was sure it wasn't mere chance. I was deliberately being prevented from talking to him. It was as if they were dancing around me in a tight cluster — Zampini,

Adeline, Giles . . . and Philip. They knew that I knew all about them. But they also knew there wasn't a thing I could do about it.

After all, what could I do? I always came back to that. What the devil could I do? I had no proof. Nothing that I could say would carry any weight against the fierce denials of these four. And if I became too troublesome . . . With a shudder I remembered what had happened to Carlo.

Get out of here — that was the only thing. Get out and stay out. And if more suckers came here begging on their knees to be rooked — well then, who was I to play guardian angel?

I caught Adeline just coming down from her siesta.

"Can I talk to you please, Miss Harcourt?"

She gave me a swift, cool, serious look. "Very well, darling." She threw open the dining-room door. "There is nobody in here."

Inside, not sitting down, I faced her. "I think I'd better go, Miss Harcourt. Back to London."

She was silent, watching me gravely. If

she had pressed me to stay, I might have weakened. I believe that if I had seen fear in her eyes again, as I had seen it before, I would have yielded.

At last Adeline nodded. "Perhaps it would be for the best. You have been unhappy here . . . "

"It's not that, Miss Harcourt," I protested.

But she didn't want to know what it was. She accepted my decision, and rushed on to planning my departure.

"We must book a flight for you. When do you want to go?"

Somehow, now that I had definitely decided on going, it seemed undignified to hustle off at once.

"I . . . I don't want to let you down," I stammered. "Perhaps the day after tomorrow."

"Leave it to me, Kerry darling I will arrange it."

Suddenly Adeline switched on her most radiant smile. And irresistible smile. "You must enjoy yourself while you remain here. I want you to have some happy memories of Sicily. It is a beautiful island."

"Yes. I could have enjoyed it so much if only . . . "

"I understand." Her voice was wistful now, heavy with a sort of yearning. "I did think that perhaps with you here . . . But there it is — you are going."

"What were you about to say, Miss Harcourt?"

I don't think she heard me. Her eyes were far away. Was she looking to the past, or to the future?

She snapped back to the present with a voice that was full of harsh self-condemnation. "I have not your courage . . . "

I hesitated. Then, watching her face, I said simply: "But I am running away, Miss Harcourt."

"Perhaps that is what I must do too, my dear. I have been so happy here, but . . . "

Was she telling me she wanted to break with Zampini? Was leaving Sicily the only way she dared break with him?

"Will you return to England, do you think?" I asked her.

She was smiling again, but sadly now. A slow smile that accepted the crueller facts of this world. "I think not. A long life has taught me never to go back. But then, I believe I could be contented anywhere as long as I have people around me."

Where was the great actress now? This was an old woman speaking from the heart.

Adeline had recovered her usual composure by teatime. She presided, a hostess in absolute command.

"I have sad news for you all," she announced, pouring tea delicately. "Our dear Kerry is to leave us."

Zampini looked up sharply. He uttered just a single word.

"When?"

"The day after tomorrow. She is quite adamant."

He nodded, eyes narrowed, thoughtful. He didn't ask why I was going.

Nor did Philip. He looked at me and then looked at Adeline. He was clearly surprised, but also . . . ? Relieved perhaps; glad to see the back of me? Or was he planning to go himself, now that Rosalind Blunt had departed?

The Austrian honeymooners were there too, They nodded and smiled, only half understanding what had been said about me.

Foolishly, I felt sorry for myself. Who minded if Kerry Lyndon went or stayed? Who cared so much as a two-penny damn? Ridiculous tears pricked behind my eyelids. Opening my bag, I searched for a handkerchief as an excuse to keep my eyes down, away from them all. I blinked hard.

The scrap of pale blue paper in the mirror pocket caught my eye at once. The printing stood out, black and clear; an advertisement for the Greek Theatre at Syracuse. Adeline had talked of taking me there. But how had the leaflet found its way into my handbag?

There was writing on the reverse side, and my eyes took in the first few words. Hastily, I thrust the paper underneath the general debris and snapped my bag closed. Through my lashes I glanced round at the others. Had I been observed?

Philip was watching me. Zampini and Adeline were laughingly trying to explain to the little Austrian couple about my going away. They were off too, tomorrow.

I had read enough of the note to make me want to get out of this room. I needed to be alone to read the rest of the message.

The words I'd seen were heavily underscored. *'Destroy this immediately you have read it'*.

I sat there gripping the clasp of my handbag, unable to keep it shut tight enough for my comfort. It was just as if that piece of paper had come to life, writhing to get out and show itself.

How to escape from one of Adeline's formal teatime sessions? How to slip away without arousing suspicion? I couldn't wait. I had to see the rest of the note. I had to know at once who had written it.

Philip? Could it be Philip? I glanced at him again, quickly. His eyes skipped away a soon as they met mine.

I stood up, handbag clutched hard to my chest. "Please forgive me, but suddenly I've got quite a bad headache ... " It sounded so lame, so horribly obvious. Like a guilty couple at a hotel desk having no better name than 'Smith' to give the reception clerk!

But they all showed concern for me. Philip jumped up. Zampini muttered sympathetically about the oppressive heat. Adeline asked if I had aspirin.

"Why don't you go and lie down, darling?"

The very second my bedroom door had closed behind me, I snatched the note out of my bag. My eyes flew to the bottom . . .

Giles!

I read so fast that the words jumbled, making no sort of sense. I had to go back and take it more slowly.

The situation is very serious. If I don't get help, my life is in danger. You and Rainsby can save me. Please meet me at noon tomorrow in the hills at Savigo, where the two roads meet. Rainsby will find it on the map. I beg you not to fail me. Do not tell anybody else.

Thrusting through my fear, racing alongside my urge to help Giles, was a tremendous joy. *You and Rainsby!* So Philip wasn't one of the gang. Giles' letter made it clear that Philip was on my side.

Impulsively, I wanted to go to him

and start making plans right away. But I had to be cautious. Zampini would be full of suspicion if he saw us putting our heads together. Philip and I had always shown a marked coolness towards one another and it was vital to keep this up.

I had to preserve the letter until I'd shown it to Philip, so we could work out the meeting place on the map. And for another reason, too. Just as I'd not trusted Philip until now, it was pretty obvious he hadn't trusted me either. To go to him with a story about getting a secret appeal from Giles would hardly invite belief. I needed that letter to convince Philip I was speaking the truth.

I didn't dare keep it in my handbag any longer. That was too vulnerable a place. Feeling rather absurd I folded the letter up small and tucked it firmly into my bra.

It was well after dinner before I was given a chance to speak to Philip alone. As earlier when Giles was here, everybody seemed to be clinging together. I was beginning to get desperate.

At last Zampini suggested to Adeline

that they play a hand of Bezique outside in the evening cool. He turned to Philip and me with an apologetic smile. "You will not object. I know you young people do not care for card playing."

"Please carry on," said Philip affably.

Adeline and Zampini settled themselves down at one of the little round tables on the loggia and within a few minutes appeared to be engrossed in their game. But both Philip and I were still in full view if they chanced to look up. I had to box it cleverly.

Discreetly, I fished for Giles' letter, and held the tight folded paper concealed in my palm. Then I lolled back comfortably on the sofa and flicked through a glossy magazine, waiting for my chance.

The magazine itself gave me a lead. Across the centre-spread was a colour splash of Etna in full eruption.

In a voice designed to carry clearly to the pair outside, I said casually: "This would interest you, Mr. Rainsby. A marvellous photograph of Etna . . . "

Plastering over his surprise with an expression of polite enquiry, Philip came across to me. I held the magazine up, with

Giles' letter opened out and pinned under my thumb for him to see.

Philip caught on immediately. "Oh yes, may I look?" Smoothly, he took the magazine from me, his thumb replacing mine as a clamp.

He stood above me, intent. Grabbing myself another glossy from the table, I flipped over a few pages. From the corner of my eye I watched Philip screw up the letter into a ball and slip it into his side pocket.

Hitching his trousers he sat down beside me, still holding the magazine open. "I hope I'm not around the next time Etna blows her top like that." He dropped his voice to a friendly murmur. "How did you get the letter?"

I explained, briefly.

He reflected. "Has Adeline told you any more since last night?"

"You believe me now? You believe Adeline did tell me all those things?"

"Never mind that for the moment." He turned a page of the magazine, keeping up the act. "Do you want to go to meet Giles?"

That took me by surprise. "Of course I

do," I hissed under my breath. "He needs help."

"You don't know what you'd be involving yourself in."

"I don't care. If Giles' life is in danger, then we've got to do everything we can."

I'd said 'we'. I'd been taking Philip's agreement for granted. He wasn't over fond of Giles, I knew, but surely he couldn't refuse to help him in these circumstances?

I realised I'd only been thinking as far as this point — of getting Philip alone and showing him the letter. I hadn't considered the problem beyond that. Now I could see the difficulties.

My face was stiff with the effort of forced smiling.

"Won't it look suspicious if we go off together?"

"Why should it? What more natural than for me to ask you out? They've probably been wondering why I didn't get around to it sooner." He flashed a quick grin at me. "Don't worry, I'll fix it."

But there was still one thing, I'd kept back and without knowing that, Philip couldn't appreciate the possible dangers of the situation. It was only fair to tell him now, before he got involved any deeper.

"Adeline said something else, Philip. Something I didn't tell you . . . "

"What is it?"

"About Carlo."

"What about him?"

"She thinks it wasn't a vendetta killing, like the police said. She thinks Zampini had him killed."

The skin around Philip's eyes was still crinkled in a friendly smile, but I could see a cold glint way back in the dark pupils.

"She's not the only one to think that, Kerry," he said slowly. "I do, as well."

14

ETNA smoked sullenly into the brassy morning sky.

For a while we had edged our way around the volanco's skirt before striking north into wild secret hills. I was glad to turn my back upon Etna.

The lesser mountains lay before us like stiff crumpled paper, roughly smoothed, burned to pale straw by the savage sunheat.

Philip had worked out our route in advance. He soon found the minor road, little more than a dusty track, that struck off to the right. We climbed steadily, winding through a scrub-filled valley, a brooding, baking wasteland.

Getting away from the villa had been surprisingly easy. At breakfast Philip had strolled across to our table on the loggia. He gave Adeline a winning smile.

"I wonder whether Miss Lyndon would care to come for a bit of a drive with me? This is, if you can spare her."

"How nice!" Adeline glanced at me with an exaggerated head-on-one-side archness. But I was glad to see this reaction. If she imagined Philip was merely inviting me out because he found me attractive, then so much the better.

"You're sure you don't mind, Miss Harcourt?"

"I'm delighted for you to have fun, Kerry darling. And for goodness' sake don't hurry back — not in this heat."

The moment we were alone together in the car I'd asked Philip the question that had refused to leave my mind all night.

"What makes you suspect Zampini was responsible for Carlo's death?"

"Just a hunch."

But I knew he was being evasive.

"It's more than that," I pressed. "You've got a good reason for thinking so, haven't you?"

The rear wheels scrabbled loosely on the dusty surface for a moment as we took a bend that was sharper than it looked.

"I don't know anything for sure, Kerry."

"But you do know more than you've admitted to me," I said sharply. We were in this thing together now, and I didn't see why he shouldn't come clean. "When you tried to make out I was talking nonsense yesterday morning — you knew it was all true, didn't you?"

He nodded. "Yes."

"So why . . . ?"

He didn't answer, as if he needed to give all his attention to the narrow winding road.

"I asked you a question, Philip."

Reluctantly, he said at last: "I wanted to protect you."

"But I knew what they were up to. How were you protecting me by refusing to believe me? By pretending I'd got it all wrong?"

His answer, if it could be called an answer at all, was very oblique. "Yorke is obviously pretty scared. Look at the care he's taken to stop them discovering that he's contacted us."

"What's it all about, Philip? Why did Carlo have to be killed? And why is Giles so scared? It isn't as though they were involved is something really serious . . . "

"Don't you think art forgery is serious?"

"Oh, of course I do! But . . . well, as

Adeline herself pointed out, the buyers ask for it, really. It only works because they all think they are cheating her, instead of the other way round . . . "

I dried up. Philip was looking so grim. "You're on dangerous ground, Kerry. If you really believe what you're saying, then you could justify every confidence trick that's ever been pulled."

"I know you're right in a way, but it isn't exactly the end of the world. There's a lot worse crimes perpetrated every day. I still can't see why they're so . . . *desperate* about it."

"It could be . . . " said Philip in a voice of quiet foreboding. "It could well be that they've got something to be desperate about."

"What are you trying to say?"

He shook his head. "I was just pointing out that if people take desperate measures, it's a pretty safe bet that they've got good cause."

I couldn't get him to say any more. I guessed the antagonism and suspicion between us these last few days had bitten too deep. Philip still wasn't ready to trust me completely.

For some distance the valley had been steadily narrowing. Now it looked as if we were coming up against a blank wall of stark brown mountain. But as we got nearer I saw that the road began a crazy zigzag ascent, a narrow twisting ribbon that was the only man-made thing in all this brutal landscape.

For a while we drove through a deep channel hewn into bare rock. Then suddenly, on our left, the ground fell away steeply. The road ahead curved to the right, following round the hillside. Philip edged back the throttle slightly and we coasted into the bend.

The drop to our left wasn't quite as sheer as I'd first thought. But even so it was steep enough, sliding away down for what looked like hundreds of feet of rocky savagery.

"It would be awkward," Philip observed mildly, "if we met something coming down the road."

There wasn't really much danger of that. For miles we hadn't seen another car, even another human being. Giles had certainly chosen well for a meeting he wanted to keep absolutely secret!

Smoothly Philip eased the car round the long curve, careful to avoid any harsh braking. The loose surface looked wickedly dangerous.

And then with a sharp crack we were out of control. The car lurched into the rockface on our right, scraping violently against it. The rear tyres lost their grip, and we were slithering sideways across the width of the road.

There was nothing I could do but hold on. It seemed inevitable that we should be flung over the cliff to an absolutely certain death.

Somehow Philip held the car on that narrow ledge of road. By a miracle of driving he countered every terrifying skid and came to a stop only inches from the edge. He pulled on the handbrake and cut the ignition.

But the mountain had the last word. There was a curious protesting noise and very slowly I felt the car heel over. It was only a slight movement but so amplified by my frightened mind that it seemed the whole mountainside was on the move.

Then with a thud we hit firm ground again. We were poised on the very edge, one wheel right over. In the stillness we could hear dislodged chunks of rock scrambling away down the steep slope.

"Quick," said Philip, clutching my arm. "Get out before some more give way."

I didn't argue. With the car leaning at such an angle it wasn't so easy, but Philip gave me a hard shove. Then he climbed out himself.

Together, we backed to the safety of the rock wall behind us.

"What . . . what happened?" I asked shakily.

"God knows! I think a tyre must have burst." He laid a protective arm around my shoulder, and oddly his gesture made me tremble more violently than ever. I'd managed to keep a grip on myself so far. Now I felt like breaking down and crying.

Philip sensed my weak knees and his arm tightened. "Sit down for a bit," he said gently. "You'll feel better in a minute."

We sat there on the hot dusty surface of the road and stared at one another in silence. We were grateful to be alive at all. For the moment we didn't think beyond that. We weren't worrying about what to do next.

The car didn't shift again. Presumably it had found the one weak spot on the rocky verge and was settled down now. But even if it wasn't going to topple over, neither could Philip and I hope to get it back on the road. That job would need a lot of help — a tractor maybe, or several men and a strong rope.

Already, in those few minutes out of the car, the sun had become our enemy. It pulsed above us, filling the entire sky with its stridency, seeming to reach out vicious claws.

The air all around vibrated with the metallic resonance of thrusting insect life. Close by, a tiny lizard darted out, a quick startled scurry. With a flick of the tail it was gone again, back to its crevice in the rocks. Maybe it had seen us, or maybe the vindictive sun was too much even for a lizard.

I wished we could find some shade so easily.

Philip got to his feet. "The map's in the glovebox. It'll help fix just exactly where we are."

"You mustn't go near the car!" I jumped up quickly, afraid for him. Any small movement might upset such a precarious balance.

Philip turned back to me. "Don't worry, Kerry. She's well bedded down now."

"Please . . . !"

He waved aside my protests. "But we need that map. I'll just open the door and reach inside. Then if the car does start sliding, all I have to do is let go."

He pretended it was as simple as that, but I felt petrified. The map wasn't very encouraging. It was too small a scale for us to pinpoint where we were to within a mile or two. But clearly, unless we were lucky enough to get a lift, we had a long walk ahead of us. The place Giles had asked us to meet him was about nine miles further on.

We decided to go back. The thought of tramping that long dusty road in the ever-mounting heat appalled me. But staying here was senseless. It was probable that no other vehicle would come this way for ages.

There was a flask of coffee in the car, but I wouldn't allow Philip to get it. I wasn't going to let him take the risk a second time.

"After all," I said decidedly, "it's not as if we were in a desert. At the very worst two or three hours' walking will get us somewhere."

Philip looked at me strangely, as if he had a foreboding that our escape was not going to be so easy. Then he switched mood, smiling cheerfully and taking my arm.

"Let's get going, then."

But we weren't to get very far. As we started round the bend, back the way we had come, a spurt of dust jumped in the road by Philip's feet. A sharp crack came almost simultaneously.

We stopped dead. The crack was repeated, echoing at us from the opposite side of the valley. And then silence. Even the insects were quiet.

Philip sprang alive. He dragged me down, hard against the rock wall.

"That was a bullet," he yelled. "Somebody's shooting at us."

15

THERE were no more shots.

Philip and I were crouched in the minimal shelter of a small rock projection. It offered no shade; just a shield between us and anybody looking down from the hillside above.

We waited for minutes on end for a sign of life, a movement. But nothing happened. The myriad insects started their strumming again; maybe they had never really stopped, and it was only my shocked brain that had registered silence. Now their noise was irksome, because we had to strain to hear the possible sound of a footfall.

The heat was almost beyond bearing. The hot rock was scorching my bare arm where I pressed against it. There was no air to breathe. I had to check myself from fainting, fighting off attacking waves of nausea.

At last Philip muttered: "We've got to get out of this. We certainly can't stay here."

"But . . . who is it?" I whispered. "Why shoot at us?" His voice was grim. "God knows! It could be bandits, I suppose."

I'd read about the lawless men of Sicily who took to the hills. I had thought they were legend, but now I was faced with the reality. I shivered violently.

"Or it might be Giles . . . " Philip said under his breath.

"*Giles!*"

"It could be. The letter — maybe it was a trap to get us out here."

I felt stunned. "But why . . . ?"

"He is one of the gang, after all. Maybe he thinks we know too much already. It might even have been Giles who did for Carlo."

"Oh no! I can't believe it. Not Giles . . . "

Philip said quietly: "Well somebody's after us, Kerry, that's for sure. And we've got to get away somehow."

"What can we do?" I asked hopelessly.

"We'll have to make a run for it."

"But the minute we stand up we'll be an easy target."

Still crouching, Philip turned his head, looking back along the curving road. "No,

I don't think so. I reckon that gunman's working his way round so as to take us by surprise. If we run hell for leather down the road, we should stand a fair chance of getting away."

It sounded horribly risky. But then so it was staying where we were. I decided I'd rather be shot taking some sort of action, than be picked off like a sitting rabbit.

"All right, Philip."

"That's my girl!" His hand gripped mine. "When I give the okay, we'll stand up together and belt off as hard as we can go."

For a hundred yards we ran like mad. Nothing happened; no more shots; no sound of running feet in pursuit. I began to think that maybe we were going to get clear away, after all. And we might have done, too, if I hadn't caught the heel of my left sandal on a big stone and ripped it clean off.

The heel had only been about an inch high, but without it I was crippled, cut to half speed. And I wouldn't last a dozen steps barefoot on this stony surface.

"Oh Philip, I'm terribly sorry . . . !" I

felt as if I were criminally responsible. This might cost us our slender chance of safety.

He wasted no time on reproaches. "Never mind that. Give me the other shoe, quickly."

Wondering, I watched him hitch the heel over a sharp edge of rock and rip it off with a single pull.

He thrust the shoe back at me. "At least they match now."

I was able to run again. Not so well as before. But stumbling, I got along at a fair pace.

The delay had been too long, though. Maybe half a minute — thirty agonising seconds. The gunman had caught up with us.

I felt a swift searing pain in my right calf. The crack of the gun came after.

The bullet ricocheted, whining on its way. But Philip didn't realise it had struck me first. Though I yelled pretty sharply, he must have put that down to the state of my nerves.

He didn't waver an instant. Without a word he plunged straight over the edge, taking me with him. For horrible seconds it was like jumping into space without a parachute. Then we hit ground.

I don't know how I managed to bottle up shouts of pain as Philip dragged me down the terrifying slope that swept all the way to the valley far below us.

The surface was rough, pitted with tricky crevices, strewn with boulders. The scrubby, heathery growth caught at our feet.

I followed Philip's lead, twisting with him, jumping with him. I gave up wondering if I would fall, abandoning myself to the mad scramble.

We had to go on, because there was terror behind us; a man with a gun. And we had to go on anyway because we couldn't stop. Our momentum was too great, the slope too steep.

How far it was I don't know. I was numb with pain and fear and exhaustion long before there came a sudden levelling out. It was only a shelf really, but wide enough to bring our headlong rush to a halt.

I tumbled to the ground, flat out. Sharp thorns needled through the thin cotton of my slacks, but that was nothing to the pain from my injured leg. I hid my face in my hands and fought off the agony. It subsided slowly, the bouncing throbs getting mercifully smaller each time.

Philip still had no idea I'd been hit, and how could I tell him now? I'd been liability enough already. He'd have got away easily by himself. I was just a drag.

The heat was terrible. The ringing sun was king, the warm-soup air cowed into utter stillness.

Standing above me taking stock, Philip grunted. "At least we shall hear him if he tries to come down after us."

"He won't need to come down here," I said tonelessly. "He could just pick us off from where he is."

"I don't think so." Philip shook his head. "There's a bit of a hump in the ground. You can't actually see the road from this spot."

"So what are we going to do?" I hardly cared any more, though. Left to myself, I would just have allowed things to happen to me, because I no longer had the will or the strength to make an effort. Despite the gravity of our position, despite my pain, I knew I could easily have put down my head and slept. I gave an enormous yawn.

Luckily, Philip didn't notice. "We'd better get moving again," he said doubtfully. "We'll try following this ledge around the hillside, and see where it leads us."

"Okay."

What did it matter, one way or another? Staying put or pressing on to . . . where?

Philip reached out a hand to give me a lift up. I bent my right leg and took my weight on it.

The pain nearly knocked me out. Starting at the wound in my calf it seemed to be splitting me open, right through my leg, all the way up the side of my body.

I fell back to the ground with a sharp yelp. I couldn't help it. I hadn't wanted Philip to know I'd been hurt, and the damage seemed so slight — scarcely more than a graze. How was it possible for a mere scratch to cause so much trouble?

Now there was no hiding it. Philip had seen that I'd nearly passed out.

"What's the matter, Kerry?" He crouched down, looking at me anxiously.

I tried to laugh it off. "Sorry to be so silly. My leg's gone a bit stiff . . . "

"Let me see."

It looked so small. A slight tear in my slacks, the frayed edges stained dark with blood. Philip enlarged the tear a bit, enough to see through to the wound.

"That's nasty. How did it happen?"

I had to tell him. "It could barely have touched me," I added lightly.

He looked serious. "You're not going to be able to walk far on that, my girl. And we need some water to clean it up."

Water! In this desert! The very shape of the word made me long for a drink. I'd not realised how ragingly thirsty I was.

I pushed the tantalising thought towards the fringe of my mind. "I'll be able to manage," I told Philip, "once I'm up on my feet."

He looked dubious, but gave me a hand up. He must have realised there was simply nothing else for it.

We started off with his arm tight around my waist, and me clutching his neck. I did a sort of hop with my bad leg and after a few yards the pain began to ease off slightly.

But only slightly. Obviously it had been a great mistake to rest, even for those few minutes. I should have kept straight on going.

We staggered over the rough ground. Every step was a big effort, every few yards a triumph. We followed the flat ledge in the mountainside for maybe five hundred yards. But then it petered out, lost in the general fall of the terrain.

We'd have to go all that way back! Trek those five hundred yards in reverse and try the opposite direction.

But even this daunting prospect would get us nowhere. "It's worse still round there," Philip explained. "That's why I chose this way."

So I just stood and waited for him to decide what to do. This time I dared not sit down. I tried to put all my weight on the uninjured leg.

Suddenly Philip exclaimed. "Look! There's a stream."

"Where?" I cried excitedly.

He pointed down the hillside. Far below us I caught a glint of silver, like a tiny thread in the drab brownness.

It was a bitter disappointment. The

thought of that distant river, water within sight and yet so mockingly out of reach, was almost more than I could bear right then.

"It's hopeless," I said in a flat voice. "We'll never get down there."

An insidious idea began to grow in my mind. It offered more than a vain hope of water; it offered me a chance to rest. Selfishly, I wanted rest above anything else.

"You go down," I suggested eagerly. "Then you could bring me . . . "

I didn't get any further. Philip shook his head decisively. "And leave you here alone? What would I fetch water in, anyway?"

He had me there.

Philip was already working out how to get me down that killing slope. "I'll have to go in a sitting position, feet first. Then if you get behind me with your legs round my waist, you can walk on your hands and do a sort of waddle." He glanced at me anxiously. "I'm afraid it'll be grim for you, Kerry. But I just can't see any other way. I couldn't possibly carry you, because it's too steep."

"I'll be okay," I said, trying to sound stoical.

Slowly, laboriously, we made our way down. We must have looked absurd. It took us all of half an hour to reach the bottom. My hands, revolting against such abuse, were raw and bleeding. My clothes were filthy and dark with sweat. I felt a hole gaping in the seat of my blue stretch pants.

I was past caring about trifles. Reaching the water made up for everything. It was no more than a stream, barely three feet across, though the dried up mud on either side showed it could be a massive river in the rainy season.

Sweet and clean, the water tasted delicious. I filled my cupped hands three times over before Philip stopped me.

"Go easy! We must see to that leg now. You can drink all you want in a minute."

Tenderly, he eased up the slacks so that my calf was exposed. The damage was certainly much more than a graze; I marvelled it had bled so little. The flesh looked ugly, with bluish-black bruising over a wide area.

Philip shook out his handkerchief and dipped it into the stream. At first touch the water was too shockingly cold, but soon the coolness of it soothed the pain. Philip bathed the wound with matter-of-fact thoroughness. He stood up suddenly and ripped of his white shirt. Before I could say a word to stop him, he had started tearing it up into strips.

"But you shouldn't have ... " I protested.

"That leg's got to be covered," he said shortly. Then he grinned. "Anyway a white shirt makes us too conspicuous. Come along now — rest it up here, and I'll bandage it for you."

I watched his face as he worked, intent upon the job in hand. His fingers deftly twisted the improvised bandage around my leg and fixed it. Then stretching the material of my slacks to the fullest extent, he worked the trouser leg down again.

"There," he said, patting my ankle gently. "How does that feel?"

"Fine," I told him. But I was lying. The leg felt a mite better, but it did not feel fine.

Philip had a drink himself then, and

afterwards he stayed kneeling, staring down into the flowing water.

"I reckon the best thing is to follow the stream. We're bound to get somewhere in the end."

It was surprising how much hope that idea gave me. For the first time since the firing of the shots, I began to think it might really be possible for us to get clear away.

I lifted my head and looked upwards, back at the mountain we had descended so wearily. Now that we had reached the floor of the valley we could see right to the top, past the hump that had obstructed our view from the ledge.

Way up something glinted in the sun. Something bright. It took a few seconds before I guessed what it was — the chromium wheelhubs of the car.

And then, way back along the road, I noticed a tiny black shape. It moved slightly as I watched. A man, walking. A man walking away from us!

I touched Philip's arm and whispered just as though I might be overheard. "Look! Up there."

His eyes took the long focus, searching

the wild expanse of mountain. Then he too caught the movement.

"Yes, it must be. Who else would be walking in this heat?"

"He's moving away, Philip.Does that mean he's given up?"

"Let's hope so! I suppose he's lost track of us. We'd better keep absolutely still until he's out of sight."

So we stayed just where we were, not daring to move. The quiet air, quivering with heat, played tricks on us, making the tiny figure on the road above dance uncertainly. Sometimes we thought he'd finally gone and then he would flicker back into existence again, moving with infinite slowness.

At last the distance had swallowed him. Our enemy was out of sight. We could get going.

Or rather, we were free to get going. When I tried to heave myself up, I found that despite Philip's careful bathing and bandaging, my leg was still in a pretty bad way.

But I wasn't going to be a burden to him any longer — not if I could help it! I grit my teeth and fought back at the fearful thumps of pain. I swear I didn't give so much as the smallest gasp as I stood up. I even forced a smile.

I might possibly have got away with it too, if Philip hadn't anticipated trouble. He was watching me far too closely to miss the obvious signs.

"Pretty rough, is it?" His voice was soft, full of anxious sympathy. "Hold on tight to me, and put as little weight on that leg as you can manage."

And so we went back to the three-legged routine. A step with my good leg and a sort of hop with the other. Philip matched me, steering me through a maze of boulders that littered the dried-up river bed. Because he had to pay attention to the ground immediately ahead he couldn't see my face, and that was a blessing.

A soft patch of ground almost toppled me over and I let out an unguarded cry.

Philip halted. "Come on, I'm going to carry you."

"But ... but you can't. I mean, we don't know how far ... "

"It'll give you a rest for a bit, anyway. Up with you."

I was ashamed to be such an encumbrance but Philip just hoisted me up, protests and all, slinging me across his shoulder in a fireman's lift.

I'd never been a skinny-lizzie. As a boy-friend of mine had once crudely put it, I was a hundred and twenty pounds of solid woman!

Philip carried my weight without a murmur. On such rough ground he couldn't avoid stumbling, and once or twice I began to slide off his shoulder. He had to stop and hump me up again.

Doubled over, hanging limply, my vision was restricted. An upside-down view of caked river mud, and a close-up of Philip's dirt-streaked back. I could see the beads of sweat forming, clinging to down-soft hairs before they shook free and hurried away along the brown channel of his spine.

Philip didn't speak much, barely more than an occasional grunt to ask if I was okay. As for me, I was glad enough to grab at this chance to rest. And anyway, humped over his shoulder, talking was a pretty jerky, breathless business.

Even in this odd and uncomfortable position, the steady jogging motion was curiously soothing. I found myself nodding off, half-way to sleep, in a sort of suspended dream world.

The sudden shade came as a shock. The air was immediately cooler, the savagery of the sun gone.

I struggled to full consciousness. "What's happened?"

"We're in a sort of gorge," Philip panted. "Where the river has cut through the rock."

I twisted my head to look sideways and up. A wall of rock rose high above us. I craned my neck the other way and saw the same thing there.

Philip pushed on for another fifty yards or so, and then stopped. Gently, he began easing me off his shoulder.

"We'll take a breather."

The difference in temperature between this shadowed place and the glaring outside world was staggering. We had flopped down beside the stream. I at once slipped off my shoes and dabbed my toes in the flowing water.

"Good idea!" Philip copied me, hitching

up his trouser legs and pulling off his shoes and socks.

It was blissful to be sitting here in deliciously cool shade. Harsh reality took some time to return.

Philip was lying back limply. He looked grey with exhaustion. I had to face the fact that, however much he might protest, we couldn't go on like this. He would pretty near kill himself if he attempted to lug me any further.

16

I KNEW what I had to say. I said it quickly, before I could weaken.

"You go on alone, Philip. I'll be okay here, and you can get help."

It sounded like false heroics. But really it was the only answer.

Philip wouldn't listen. "No, I couldn't possibly do that, Kerry."

I pitied him. I suppose it's always tough for a man to accept physical defeat. But Philip must accept it now if we were to stand a dog's chance of getting back to safety.

Nobody except Giles had the faintest idea where we might be. And where did Giles stand?

Was Philip's guess right? Had Giles sent that letter as a trick? Had he craftily manoeuvred to get us out here in the wilds where we could be ruthlessly shot down?

I still refused to believe it. But even if Giles was on the level, if that note meant what it said, then he was desperately afraid for his own skin. Was he likely to come searching for us? Was he likely even to report us missing? Would he risk the story coming out of how we got to be lost in this remote place?

I faced Philip with a brutal frankness. "You can't carry me any further," I said quietly, "and you know it. You've just got to leave me and go for help. It's the only hope for both of us."

"But Kerry . . . "

"*Please* Philip!"

"How the devil can I leave you alone here?" he asked me reproachfully. "We'll rest for a bit and then I'll be all right."

"No."

At last I got him to see the light. Or at any rate he understood that I was adamant.

After a pause he said thoughtfully: "We must find a spot where you aren't in full view of . . . of anyone coming this way."

There were plenty of hiding places in the gorge. Cracks in the rocky sides as big as caves: clusters of boulders making ideal niches where I could stay concealed. I would really be impossible for one man to make a thorough search of them all.

Philip took his time about finding the best position. Finally he selected a pile of rocks forming a rough horseshoe. Lying or sitting in the hollow centre, I should not be visible to anyone coming through the gorge. But it was conveniently close to the stream, and that was important. We had nothing to store water in, and if Philip was gone for some hours I should need a drink.

"I must be sure I can recognise the place again," Philip said as he made me comfortable.

"You don't have to worry about that. I'll give you a shout."

"But you might be asleep," he pointed out. I knew what he really meant was that I might not still be conscious.

I wanted to ask him how long he thought he'd be gone, but I said nothing. It would seem as if I were putting pressure on him to hurry. I knew anyway that he would drive himself to the limit to avoid keeping me waiting a single unnecessary minute.

There was no further excuse for Philip to delay going. He gazed down at me unhappily. "I'll be as quick as I can, but . . . " He stopped short, and then said abruptly: "For God's sake don't show yourself if you hear anyone coming . . . "

Suddenly he was kneeling beside me, his hands stroking my hair. Leaning forward he kissed me softly upon the lips.

And then he was gone, scrambling away over the rocks. I strained to hear his footsteps until I could no longer be sure the faint sounds were not just in my imagination.

It was utterly quiet in the gorge. Now I was resting the pain in my leg had subsided to a dull throb that I could forget for seconds at a time. My thoughts flitted butterfly-like, sheering away timidly from the unpleasant and the frightening; hovering gently over the memory of Philip's kiss.

I drifted into a sort of golden delirium. I was building gossamer castles in the air, a hazy future in which Philip was the one solid fact.

Philip . . .

A distant noise cracked the silence. It pierced my mind, startling me without having any particular meaning. But a repetition, and then a third time, brought home its significance with a vengeance.

It was a gun again. A tremor shook me violently.

We had watched our unknown enemy go off in the opposite direction. But he could easily have turned back. He'd not been weighed down like Philip with my dead weight, and would have covered the ground far more quickly. And most likely it was territory he knew well anyway.

Three shots! Was there a hope that Philip had escaped unhurt? And if by some miracle he had, then there would be more shots, and more. In the end he would be tracked down and killed.

My tortured mind pictured Philip's body lying among the scattered boulders of the dried-up river bed.

There was absolutely nothing I could do. Nothing! With my leg injured, I doubted if I'd get even fifty yards. And in any case, as soon as I emerged from hiding the gunman would be able to pick me off at his leisure. Not that I'd care, now that Philip was dead.

I didn't notice the passing of time until

I saw that the sun was sliding an edge of harsh light down that opposite wall of rock, inch by inch. Soon, I calculated, the scorching rays would touch the floor of the gorge and begin creeping towards the stream.

I shrunk back, cowering deeper into the shade. I was terrified at the thought of being exposed to the sun in the full blasting heat of afternoon. My thin clothes offered no protection at all.

I'd have to change my hideout, I decided. The only certain shade that I could see was behind me, right up against the wall of the gorge and far away from the stream. I'd take a long drink first, and then somehow get myself to the new position. Once established there, I'd have to sit it out until help came.

But help wasn't coming, so what was I thinking of . . . ?

In spite of myself, the instinct for self-preservation had taken over. In spite of myself, my mind churned with feeble plans.

I tried to stand, to walk, but the pain was too much — I very nearly passed out. I had to crawl down to the stream. On hands and knees it was only marginally easier, but I managed somehow.

A drink ladled to my lips in eager shaking hands. And then a rest before beginning the long haul to my new hiding place. Just a very short rest . . .

It was the kiss of hot sun on my shoulder that woke me. Shifting automatically from it's burning touch, I was all at once gripped by a violent, uncontrollable spasm of shivering. I observed this unaccountable behaviour of my body with a curious detachment. I held up an arm, and could actually see the fingers trembling. It was only when I raised the arm still further and touched my cheek, that I realised I was in a fever.

My fuddled brain snapped into clear focus. I wasn't going to stay here, an easy target for the mysterious gunman. Whatever it cost in effort and pain, I would find shelter. This became the sum total of my ambition — my only goal.

It probably took me fifteen minutes to crawl to a place where a cleft in the rockface offered space enough; but it seemed like hours, or even days.

The floor of my mini-cave was soft, a sandy texture. It was cool and felt slightly damp. Exhausted by my efforts I lay staring out across six feet of level ground to where a huge boulder partially blocked my view.

In one of the ruts left by my dragging legs a small horny beetle lay stranded on its back. I watched, half-mesmerised by its feeble waving legs. The little insect's life-and-death struggled became important to me. I began murmuring foolish words of encouragement . . .

The touch on my forehead was gentle. A soft stroking movement, almost a caress.

"*Philip!*"

I reached up to keep the hand there, wanting the soothing pressure to go on and on and on. But even before I touched the podgy wrist I knew it could not be Philip. Philip was dead.

I was fully awake in an instant. Fear clawed my spine, obliterating the insistent pain in my leg.

Guido Zampini was bending over me solicitously.

Almost before the question was in my

mind, I had an answer. His right hand held a gun, and though he saw my eyes were open, he still made no attempt to conceal it.

He sat back heavily against the big boulder, the gun in his lap. His light grey suit was filthy, dark-stained with sweat.

"My poor Signorina Lyndon, you are hurt," he said in breathless jerks. "I have been observing your struggles."

I said nothing. Just lay there and stared at him.

Idly, he began to twirl the gun on a fat forefinger. "Fortunately, you will not have to suffer much longer."

I shouted in a sudden burst of fury, as if violent words might wound him: "You killed Philip Rainsby! You killed Philip!"

He gave a sigh. "So much trouble it would have saved, if I had." Frowning down at the gun, he went on: "Regrettably I am out of practice with this toy, though my first bullet did locate the tyre of your automobile. That should have been sufficient, but Signore Rainsby is an excellent driver."

I dared not let myself hope. "But I heard three more shots just now."

"All missed, alas. He is a very agile young man."

In my relief I think I must have smiled at Zampini. He smiled back, but shook his head slowly from side to side. "It is of no avail, Signorina Lyndon. I cannot permit either of you to live now. You know too much about me."

But I was triumphant, forgetting my own danger. "You won't get away with it. Philip will bring help."

"I think not."

Quite lazily, without warning, he fired the gun twice. The bullets spun harmlessly off the rock high above me.

I gaped at him.

Zampini smirked complacently. "That will bring him running back to find his beloved."

Sickened, I understood what Zampini meant. If Philip heard shots now, he would know I was the victim. He would come back to find me, however slight the hope that I would still be alive.

Because I loved him, I prayed he would not come. I prayed that he was beyond the sound of those two shots.

Zampini seemed to follow by thoughts. "He will not be as far off as you think, my dear young lady. The gorge narrows further along and progress is very difficult."

I didn't reply. It was a little while before I realised that I was deliberately staying silent in order to listen the better. Above the buzz of insects and the faint ripple of the stream, I was straining to hear the first sound of Philip's approach.

The sun was now flooding the whole gorge so that only a few pools of shadow remained. The hiding place that Philip had selected so carefully was still in shade. If only I'd had the sense to remain there; if only I'd trusted Philip's judgement and not moved my position, then Guido Zampini would never have found me. He wouldn't now be sitting over me with a gun, and Philip would be safely out of his reach.

Zampini, settling himself down to wait, was nibbling his fingernails. As I watched him the idea began to grow that he was not quite as sure of himself as he pretended. I had never noticed this nailbiting before — was it a sign of nervous tension?

To bring Philip back, he had fired two aimless shots into the air. It occured to me suddenly that he might more profitably have used them for shooting me, as Philip was meant to believe. Why was Zampini keeping me alive now if he intended to kill us both eventually?

The only answer I could see was that he was afraid to kill me — yet. If he were to murder me now, and Philip got clear away, then Zampini would have my death to answer for, on top of his other crimes. But if Philip came back for me as Zampini confidently expected, then it would be easy enough to deal with us both together. Zampini had a gun; we had nothing. He would shoot us and push our bodies deep into a rocky crevice. And nobody would ever discover us. Our disappearance would remain a mystery and Zampini would be free from suspicion.

He was sitting quite still now, somnolent in the heat, his massive shoulders propped against the boulder. Astute though I knew him to be, I wondered hopefully if he would fall asleep. For such a fat man today's exertions must have been pretty tiring.

Uncannily, Zampini seemed aware of my every turn of thought. His dropping eyelids lifted, and one of them slowly closed again in a knowing wink.

In the surrounding barrenness a tiny movement registered in my brain. It jumped out at me like a familiar name on a printed page, and was at once engulfed again in the general stillness. My eyes searched for it, scanning and re-scanning close up and away across the gorge. But there was nothing to be seen. I glanced quickly at Zampini's face. He seemed not to have noticed my tense alertness.

And then, as I let my gaze wander again, I caught the movement once more. This time I pinpointed the exact spot. Some twenty feet away, beyond Zampini's left shoulder, amid the scattered boulders of the gorge.

Nothing moved now. Surely something was there, though? Surely I hadn't been mistaken a second time?

And then, as I watched, a stone shifted — a round black stone. Slowly it lifted itself three inches, and I saw the stone was a head of thick dark hair.

Another few inches, and I was looking across space into Philip's eyes.

17

HE had come back for me then! But slicing through my joy was a terrible fear, for him and for me. Zampini had his gun at the ready, and I was immobilised. If he realised Philip was there behind him, he had only to turn and take aim. He could not miss this time, not at such short range.

Philip was utterly still now. He kept his head lifted clear of the ground, obviously taking in the lie of the land. His eyes frowned a message, a warning not to do anything that might give the alarm to Zampini.

As I glanced slowly away from Philip I allowed no flicker of emotion to show on my face. Somehow I had to hold Zampini's attention, keep him involved in conversation, if Philip was to have the hope of a chance.

The words were a dry rustle in my throat as I put a random question. "Why do you want to kill us?"

"Because you are dangerous to me, my dear."

"Dangerous? How are we dangerous?" I was making myself speak louder, hoping my voice would drown any noise Philip made. "All we know is that you've been cheating over a few paintings."

"But you know more than that, I think."

Was he talking about Carlo's death? Had he somehow guessed that Adeline had told me of her suspicions? She would never have admitted so to him, I felt sure — she was too afraid of the man. In spite of her brave performance at breakfast yesterday, I was still convinced that her terror of Zampini was very real.

"Miss Harcourt confirmed what I already suspected," I went chattering on. "That you have been selling forged Raphaels at the *Villa Stella d'Oro.* If you're up to anything else as well, then I don't know about it."

He shrugged his indifference. "Even if *you* do not know, then your friend Signor Rainsby does."

"He can't do," I burst out. "He'd have told me."

But Philip hadn't told me everything he knew — he hadn't trusted me enough.

In the brief pause I heard the faint scrape of a stone. I dared not look, but I knew it must be Philip sliding cautiously nearer.

Covering the dangerous gap of quiet, I said hurriedly: "You forced poor Miss Harcourt into this scheme of yours. She's been wanting to stop."

"Forced?" he sneered. "She needed no persuasion. But Adeline must learn that she cannot just withdraw when the sport no longer amuses her."

"She is utterly terrified of you."

"Quite without cause, I assure you. That is, so long as she does what she is told — and refrains from being too inquisitive."

To my wide-stretched ears Philip seemed to be making the very dickens of a racket. Zampini was bound to hear him if he went on like that. I'd have to engage the man's interest even more closely.

"Just what is your game?" I asked loudly. "What's it all about?"

His snigger was full of self-satisfaction.

"Something very much more profitable than selling a few forged paintings, my dear lady. That serves merely as a convenient camouflage."

He looked so pleased with himself. In his desire to boast I guessed he was ready to tell me anything. Everything. And I didn't care now. I just wanted to give Philip the covering noise of conversation.

"So you're even cheating your accomplices, are you? Poor Miss Harcourt — and poor Giles Yorke too, I suppose."

"Giles tried to defraud *me* — do you know that?" His lips snarled up horribly. "He was idiot enough to imagine he could escape the consequences."

Zampini was breathing heavily, angered by the memory of whatever it was Giles had done. To add more fuel to his rage, I thrust in quickly: "I'm sure Giles never meant harm to anyone. You corrupted him."

"You want to know what he did?" Zampini spat out. "Your so innocent little English friend? Let me tell you then. Two weeks ago he dared to send away an American woman, a Mrs. Greenberg, with one of the paintings he had already done for selling to the tourists."

"But . . . but I don't understand . . . "

"You understand perfectly well," Zampini exclaimed impatiently. "Giles was supposed to paint a scene of Taormina Bay *over* the picture the woman had purchased from Adeline. But instead he gave this Mrs. Greenberg one from his stock, and kept back the 'Raphael' to save himself the trouble of painting another later on."

I was only half-listening, because I was straining hard to pick up any sign of Philip's progress. Without daring to look directly, I tried to catch a glimpse of him on the outskirts of my vision. But I could detect no movement. I didn't know where he was. I could only hope and keep Zampini talking.

What Zampini had been saying fitted in with Giles' character. Basically indolent, he'd have thought it a great lark to dodge an extra job by switching the canvases.

"How did you discover what Giles had done?"

"My contact in New York telephoned me."

That call in the middle of the night! No

wonder Zampini had been so enraged!

I kept at it: "I suppose he stripped off Giles' picture of Taormina Bay with the usual chemicals, and found there was nothing underneath?"

"How quick you are," Zampini said sarcastically.

"And he didn't know what to tell the customer?"

"He had great difficulty in convincing her that there really was nothing underneath — that he had not stolen her Raphael for himself. But he was even more concerned about getting the wrong frame . . . "

"The wrong frame?" I echoed. "Why should the frame matter so much?"

He regarded me with an almost childish leer of triumph, flushed with admiration for his own cleverness.

"Hollowed out you see, Signorina Kerry Lyndon, those frames we use can conceal almost half a kilogram of cocaine. Or heroin, or whatever the market for the moment demands."

"Drugs! So that's your racket! I might have guessed it was something pretty filthy . . . "

But Zampini was too bursting with conceit to be riled by petty insults. "An ingenious system, do you not think? Innocent tourists perform the dangerous part for us — the transportment. Always different people, you understand, so the Customs men never grow suspicious. And at the other end they cannot wait to see their beautiful 'Raphael' again. Our agent does the necessary restoration work and hands them back their painting in a frame that looks the same, but is not."

"Does Giles know about the drugs?"

Zampini's lips curled. "Now he does. It was necessary that he should understand what he is up against. Your young friend will not benefit financially, but he will be a good boy in future, I think."

No wonder Giles was terrified for his life! No wonder he'd begged us to meet him in such secrecy.

"I suppose somehow or other you found out he'd asked for our help, and followed us up here?"

Zampini's ugly face split into a cruel smile, a victorious smile. "But it was not Giles who sent you that letter — it was I."

"*You!*"

It was my first absolutely genuine reaction since I'd started this conversation. Zampini was delighted to have jerked me into such astonishment.

"I relied upon the fact that you and Signor Rainsby would not reject such a heart-rending appeal for help — not from a fellow countryman."

So Philip and I had voluntarily driven slap into Zampini's trap. We were facing death now for nothing; we hadn't even the comfort of knowing that at least we'd done our best to help Giles.

Why had I been so gullible? Why hadn't I suspected that the secret letter — a strangely stilted letter, I now realised, had not really come from Giles? I'd been revolted by Zampini since I first met him. I'd hated him, and these last two days I'd feared him too.

But I hadn't feared him enough! He was cleverer than I'd believed, more ruthless than I'd thought possible. And if he succeeded in murdering us, he would continue to exploit Adeline and Giles just as cleverly and ruthlessly.

But there was hope, for them as well as

us, if Philip managed to outwit Zampini.

I could see a moving black shape on the boulder, way above Zampini's head; a blurred shape because I dared not look directly. I knew Philip was preparing to jump our enemy. As he slowly rose to his feet, the rays of the westering sun caught his head and shoulders, laying a sparkling orange halo around them.

It was the shadow that warned Zampini — one second too soon. He swore and began scrambling heavily to his feet.

With some instinctive sixth-sense reaction I threw a joyful look sideways into blank space, and cried: "Philip . . . Oh *Philip!*"

It was enough to divert Zampini. Just as instinctively he followed my glance . . .

Philip launched himself. No trapeze artist could have been more precise. Zampini's great bulk was flattened, and Philip's foot came hard down upon the hand that held the gun.

The Italian let out a great bellow of rage, a screech of pain. And then Philip was holding the gun, pointing it at Zampini.

"Nice work, Kerry darling."

"Oh Philip . . . !"

I was going to cry. Now that the agonised waiting was over, I was going to break down and sob. I knew it.

Philip must have known it too, because he quite firmly wouldn't let me get started. "What the hell are we going to do with fatso?" he asked flippantly, and then slid me a quick. "D'you reckon we could carry him, Kerry?"

"Oh Philip . . . !" I was getting monotonous.

I couldn't take my eyes off him. He was filthy, his fawn cotton slacks ripped halfway up one leg. His back was streaked with more than dirt. He'd been bleeding quite a lot from a long gash on his left shoulder.

Astonishingly, a warm sense of well-being was swirling through me. I reckon I was still a bit delirious. I felt a queer sort of remoteness from what was going on. Philip was back. Philip was in control, and everything could be left to him to sort out.

I knew, vaguely, that I was being absurd. Philip's strength was not limitless. How could he now tackle the job of getting an injured girl and a dangerous criminal from out of this desolate back of beyond? To leave me alone again while he escorted Zampini back at gunpoint into the hands of the police was something I knew Philip wouldn't even consider. Could he tie up Zampini and leave him here to be collected later? But what would he use as cords?

It was beginning to look like stalemate. Having the weapon still didn't give us the whip hand.

I had wild notions about shooting Zampini in the leg so as to cripple him as he had crippled me. But could Philip bring himself to shoot any man in cold blood? Could I let him do it?

I forgot such a crazy idea.

Philip had ordered Zampini to sit down at a spot a few yards off. He himself was flopped beside me, glad of a rest while he considered what to do. He was giving Zampini no chance to try anything. Having checked the gun was still loaded, he was keeping the man closely covered.

"It's a good job old Guido is such a lousy shot," he observed, soft-pedalling the situation. Then he glanced at my leg. "Sorry, darling! He wasn't such a lousy shot after all. How do you feel?"

I smiled weakly. "A lot better now than I did a few minutes ago. But how on earth are we going to get out of this mess?"

"Don't worry, I'll think of something." He grinned across at Zampini. "And you'll get your just deserts, chum."

Zampini came to life suddenly, speaking for the first time. "You are a fool, Rainsby, if you imagine you can escape my . . . my friends, whatever you may do to me. They are very powerful."

"So you're not the top dog then? And just who are these wonderful friends of yours?"

But Zampini had clamped his mouth tight shut.

There was a short silence. Then, heedless that Zampini could overhear every word, I asked Philip: "Who are you really? I mean — that lame story about being an art buyer . . . "

"I'm sorry about that, Kerry, but I had to tell you something. And it wasn't so far out of line."

"Were you on to this drug trafficking all along?"

"Not me! It was the forgeries I was interested in. I work for a London gallery which specialises in the Renaissance period, and we were getting worried because of hints that fake Raphaels were being unloaded on to the market. The signs pointed to Rome as the source. Since I speak Italian I was sent out to sniff around."

"So those stories were just a cover up."

He nodded. "Carefully angled for the benefit of friend Guido and his pals. I turned up in Rome pretending to be a rep for an electrical firm, but it was discreetly leaked around that really I was a buyer for a rich American art collector. Zampini rose right up out of the water and took the bait."

Philip was talking about Zampini as though the man weren't there. The great fat body was slumped like a stranded sea lion; cowed, no longer dangerous. I think he was scarcely aware of us.

I said to Philip: "But you did know something about this drug racket, didn't you?"

"I'd begun to suspect there was more to it than the forgeries. But I didn't learn about the drugs until yesterday."

"Why didn't you tell me?"

"Because I was so scared for you, Kerry. When you come up against the drug traffic, it gets really dangerous. The less you knew about it, darling, the safer I reckoned you were."

And I'd been hurt that he hadn't trusted me!

"How was it you found out? About the drugs, I mean?"

"Pastore told me."

"Cesare . . . ?"

"That chap is more than he seems. He's quite a big fish in the Interpol narcotics squad."

"Not Inspector Vigorelli's assistant?"

Philip smiled quietly. "Like me, he needed a cover story."

"So you've been working with the police all along?"

"You wouldn't think that if you knew the way they'd had me investigated. That's how Pastore knew I was in the clear. He told me what was happening because he wanted someone to keep an eye on things at the villa. He had a hunch that the balloon was going up."

There was a sudden rustling noise, a scrabbling of loose stones. As if on cue the tall figure of Cesare Pastore rose from the ground, barely a dozen yards away.

"Forgive my unexpected appearance," he said with an apologetic grin, "but I had to be certain which of you was holding the gun before I revealed myself."

18

THE trek back took hours.

I made an awkward parcel for the two men. They chaired me between them, my arms uncomfortably hooked to their necks.

Zampini was made to walk well ahead so he couldn't try any tricks. He offered no resistance, looking forlorn and absurdly grotesque in defeat.

The sun was low now, sinking fast towards westward hills. Our shadows were long on the dry-baked ground. Following the river bed the way we had come, our tired progress became slower and slower.

Philip and I wanted to know how it was that Cesare had turned up so conveniently.

"I was on Zampini's scent," he told us. "When I found he was not at the *Villa Stella d'Oro* this morning, I made some enquiries."

"But how did you discover he'd come this way?" I asked, puzzled.

Cesare was panting a little under my weight. "You would be surprised how much is observed, even out here in the wilds."

He had recognised the car that hung poised on the edge of the mountain road. He had heard three distant shots; and then, later, two more.

"But there were no further clues," he went on. "Frankly I was wondering what I could do next."

"With equal frankness," said Philip dryly, "that is exactly what I was wondering, too."

Mercifully we were to avoid the climb back up that awful slope. Cesare knew something of the terrain, and we kept to the path of the river until finally we reached an isolated settlement — a huddle of dilapidated farm buildings. There was no telephone, and the best the willing peasants could do by way of transport was an incredibly ancient lorry. This springless box on wheels reeked of the farmyard, but I didn't care. Luxuriously I lay back on some sacking, glowing from a dose of savagely coarse red wine.

The lorry jolted noisily up the mountain

track to the point where Philip and I had so nearly pitched over the edge.

Turning Cesare's car on the narrow road was a bit of a job, and then we were continuing on our way.

Philip and I — and the gun — were in the back. Zampini overflowed the bucket seat beside Cesare.

"Better head straight for the *Stella d'Oro*," said Philip. "I want a doctor to look at that leg of Kerry's."

Cesare told us that Zampini's capture completed the rounding up of the drug ring. "We've got all the top boys now," he said with a flippancy that didn't conceal his jubilation.

Zampini shot him a look of surprise, but I thought he perked up slightly after that, as if he found the news cheering. Maybe he felt safer with his ruthless confederates no longer at large.

"It was a call for Zampini from New York that began it all," Cesare went on. "The phone at the *Stella d'Oro* was tapped, you see. Our American colleagues followed it through, and fortunately Zampini's contact over there was talkative. We got a long list of names from him."

"So that's that." Cuddled up against Philip I felt a deep contentment. I added sleepily: "And you won't have to take any action against Adeline and Giles, will you?"

Cesare threw a glance over his shoulder. "Those two have a great deal to answer for."

"But they knew nothing about the drugs . . . "

He cut across me severely. "They have been connected with a drug-smuggling organisation. That is a very serious matter. We shall need to be entirely satisfied of their innocence in this respect. And apart from that, there is no doubt they were dealing in forged paintings."

"So you *are* going to arrest them?" I cried, dismayed.

"They must certainly be taken in for questioning. What happens afterwards remains to be seen."

"But that's just plain silly. You know as well as I do that it was only a game to them." Mutinously I began wondering if there wasn't some way of warning Adeline. My hard thoughts about her were rapidly melting before a warm flow of affection. Hadn't she been most awfully kind to me?

In his official manner Cesare was saying: "Inspector Vigorelli's men will have picked up Giles Yorke by now. Signora Harcourt I shall attend to myself as soon as we get to the villa."

It was already dark when we swung into the cypress-lined drive of the *Stella d'Oro*. There were no lights showing and the front door was unexpectedly locked.

Impatiently, Cesare rang the bell. Philip stayed with me in the car, keeping Zampini covered.

There was quite a wait before we saw any sign of life. A light went on in the hall, and Maria's frightened voice asked who was there.

Cesare barked that it was the police.

The door stayed shut.

"Maria," I called gently. "It is Miss Lyndon and Mr. Rainsby."

We heard scuffling noises from inside. The door seemed to be fixed with everything Maria could lay her hands on. Not just bolts and chains; it sounded as if furniture was being shifted.

Two scared faces peered out. Maria and Luciana.

Philip lifted me out of the car and carried me up the steps straight through the hall into the salon. Carefully he put me down on a sofa. "I'm going to ring for a doctor," he said, hurrying off.

Zampini came lumbering in, prodded from behind by Cesare. He sat down where he was told on an upright chair in a corner. I asked them where Miss Harcourt was.

Maria broke into a string of fast Italian before remembering I could understand hardly a word of it. "The signora has . . . left."

"Left!" Wild hope was rising in me. "Do you mean she has gone away?"

It was more than Maria could manage in English. As Cesare translated for me his voice showed deep displeasure.

"Signora Harcourt went off about an hour ago. She drove away in her car, saying she would not be back. Apparently she told these two women they would be well looked after."

"So she's got away after all." I couldn't hold back a smile of relief. "You'll not have the chance to put the poor old thing through your beastly third degree."

"She will not get very far. Sicily is an island, remember. We shall catch up with her before long."

But I had a hunch that Adeline might prove a match for the police force. I hoped so.

The phone was busier than I'd ever known it. After Philip, Cesare got through to police headquarters. And then there was an incoming call for me.

"Your friend Miss Halliday-Browne," announced Cesare.

"*Monica!* Good heavens! Is she back in Rome?"

He shrugged indifferently, too involved with his own problems. "She did not say."

Philip solved the matter of getting me to the phone by carrying me there, just as if it were normal procedure. There was nowhere for me to sit in the little telephone room, so he stood holding me in his arms. He was still without a shirt, still dirty and bloodstreaked.

I grabbed up the receiver. "Monica! How lovely!"

Monica's delight nearly split my eardrums. "Kerry, my pet! I just had to give you a ring." But then the voice dropped and became quite different. "Please listen carefully, Kerry darling. Do not show any surprise, but act as though you really are speaking to Monica."

I choked back my astonishment and clamped the receiver tighter to my ear so Philip couldn't hear.

"Er . . . Monica, we've had an awful lot of excitement here. I must tell you all about it sometime."

Adeline sounded anxious. "But are *you* all right, Kerry? I had a dreadful fear that Guido might . . . "

"You'll never guess," I went on brightly. "That man Zampini turned out to be a dreadful crook who'd been smuggling drugs out of Sicily, and he's just been arrested . . . "

"Thank God for that! It was the only way." She hesitated. "I . . . I'm sorry to have let you down so badly, Kerry. You understand that I have to go away now? There is no alternative."

"I understand . . . Monica."

"I made my plans a long time

ago — just in case; and I told my lawyer what I wanted done with my possessions if ... if I ever left Sicily. The *Stella d'Oro* is to go to the nuns, and I have made provision for Maria and Luciana — and a bit for old Pietro. But you, Kerry darling; what will you do now?"

I looked at Philip. He leaned forward and kissed my nose. "I shall go back to London," I said into the phone. "Maybe I should have done that before, but I'm glad I didn't now."

"I must be going, Kerry darling."

"You haven't said where you are phoning from — what your plans are."

Was it a sigh at the end of the line, or was it a chuckle? I couldn't be sure. "I can't tell even you that, Kerry darling. We may meet again — who knows?"

She sounded quite cheerful, as if she were about to embark on a great adventure. Maybe that was how she thought of it.

I wanted to ask her about Giles, but I couldn't think of a way. Perhaps Adeline understood my hesitation for as an afterthought she put in: "Oh by the way, I phoned Giles to warn him, the very moment I heard."

"Oh good!" I made it sound quite matter-of-fact. "And how did you come to hear? You haven't explained that."

I glanced quickly at Philip to see if I'd said too much. I was supposed to be talking to Monica, not Adeline. But he grinned at me patiently, shifting my weight in his arms.

Poor Philip! He should be cleaned up and resting by now, not holding me while I chatted on the telephone. I hated deceiving him like this, but I wasn't yet sure about his attitude to Adeline's escape. And I might never get another chance of speaking to her.

"How *did* you know ... Monica?" I pressed.

This time it was definitely a chuckle, filled with teasing overtones. "Some men, my dear Kerry, will still put loyalty to a friend above the call of blind duty."

Suddenly I didn't want her to tell me any more. "I'm glad," I said simply, my throat oddly restricted. "And ... Monica ... "

She waited, and then prompted, "Yes, darling?"

I went on quickly, because I felt like crying: "I hope you find somewhere ... somewhere nice, very soon. And all my love."

As Philip carried me back into the salon he asked: "What on earth was all that about?"

I gulped. "Oh, you know what Monica's like — always doing things on the spur of the moment. She just wanted to say hallo, really."

A fortuitous commotion announced the arrival of both doctor and a carload of police. Inspector Vigorelli came bustling in importantly, glaring at the captive Zampini. He gave a brief nod to Cesare and then came towards me, smiling.

But there was gravity in the smile. "My dear Signorina Lyndon, I regret I bring you sad news."

"Sad news?"

"Your friend Giles Yorke is dead. He was trying to escape from my men. He jumped from the window of his studio to the rooftop, but unhappily, he slipped and fell ... "

"Oh no ... "

Cesare was scowling at the inspector.

"How is it possible that Yorke was allowed to get away? Such inefficiency!"

His cold police reaction switched my sorrow to swift anger. A man had died, and to Cesare it was a matter of reprehensible inefficiency.

Inspector Vigorelli was unruffled by the criticism. His gaze swivelled round the room until he was looking directly at Cesare, and his eyes held a challenge. "My men both went to the studio door and knocked and waited there. I . . . omitted to warn them to guard the window also . . . "

"And Signora Harcourt has escaped us too," Cesare exploded. "Do you realise that?"

Inspector Vigorelli painted surprise over his bland face. "So she has disappeared? One might imagine she received a — what is it called in English? A tip-off."

"One might suppose something of the sort." Cesare's anger was subsiding into a half-amused resignation. "Do you think if your department instituted a search for Signora Harcourt, it could hope to meet with any success?"

"We can try." Vigorelli scratched his

wiry moustache, hiding his mouth. "I shall put in hand the necessary arrangements as soon as I get back to my headquarters."

"And how soon will that be?" inquired Cesare ironically.

"Why this evening, naturally. The moment I have finished my dinner."

Cesare didn't argue any more.

Later, when Philip and I had a chance to talk alone, I tackled him about Adeline. "You're glad, aren't you, that she's managed to get away?"

"What me!" Then he laughed out loud. "It's a good job I'm not the vindictive type. At least those damned Raphael forgeries have stopped.

As the plane to Rome climbed higher I didn't trouble to look back at Etna. One day, perhaps, I'd return to Sicily. But at the moment I wanted only to get away.

The morning had been hectic, preparing to leave at such short notice. But there was really no reason for Philip and I to stay on. Between them, the police and Adeline's lawyer were coping with the problems she had left behind her.

My leg, stretched out before me on a

footrest, was feeling a whole lot better. The doctor had pronounced that there was no serious damage and that it was just a matter of time.

Philip's hand found mine. "Don't be sad, darling."

I smiled at him quickly. "But I'm not sad."

"You seem a bit wistful."

"Oh well, after all that's happened . . . "

"The Art world doesn't often provide such excitement. Will you settle down to the quiet life?"

"Just you try me!"

His arm slid around my shoulder and drew me closer. Foolishly, I felt a bit shy. I glanced round hastily to see if anyone had noticed, but none of the other passengers seemed interested in us.

Across the gangway, alone in a pair of seats, sat an elderly nun. She was placidly starting on a salad lunch, enjoying with it a small carafe of red wine.

Something about her caught my attention, yet just what it was I couldn't fathom. If ever anyone looked like a typical Mother Superior, she did. The calm relaxed profile, close encased by the stiff nun's wimple, expressed a dignity and inner beauty such as I had often seen on the screen.

Covertly, I watched her as she ate. So serenely unhurried; yet wasn't she just a tiny bit larger than life?

I realised that she, at least, was aware of Philip and me. She put down her glass, delicately, and turned her face to smile.

The disguise was perfect. Or almost perfect.

Amused lips formed the words which floated silently across the few feet separating us.

"Good luck."

I smiled back, and then flicked a look at Philip. He'd noticed nothing.

I'd tell him, of course. There was nothing I wouldn't tell Philip.

But not quite yet. Time enough when we were back in London. Time enough when Adeline Harcourt had safely disappeared into the blue.

Openly, I reached out for Philip's hand, squeezing it tightly. I thought the nun would be glad to know just how things stood between us.

I'm sure she was. The smile lingered upon her face as she returned to her luncheon tray with good appetite.

THE END

TO FIGHT THE WILD
Rod Ansell and Rachel Percy

Lost in uncharted Australian bush, Rod Ansell survived by hunting and trapping wild animals, improvising shelter and using all the bushman's skills he knew.

COROMANDEL
Pat Barr

India in the 1830s is a hot, uncomfortable place, where the East India Company still rules. Amelia and her new husband find themselves caught up in the animosities which seethe between the old order and the new.

THE SMALL PARTY
Lillian Beckwith

A frightening journey to safety begins for Ruth and her small party as their island is caught up in the dangers of armed insurrection.

NURSE ALICE IN LOVE
Theresa Charles

Accepting the post of nurse to little Fernie Sherrod, Alice Everton could not guess at the romance, suspense and danger which lay ahead at the Sherrod's isolated estate.

POIROT INVESTIGATES
Agatha Christie

Two things bind these eleven stories together — the brilliance and uncanny skill of the diminutive Belgian detective, and the stupidity of his Watson-like partner, Captain Hastings.

LET LOOSE THE TIGERS
Josephine Cox

Queenie promised to find the long-lost son of the frail, elderly murderess, Hannah Jason. But her enquiries threatened to unlock the cage where crucial secrets had long been held captive.

THE LISTERDALE MYSTERY
Agatha Christie

Twelve short stories ranging from the light-hearted to the macabre, diverse mysteries ingeniously and plausibly contrived and convincingly unravelled.

TO BE LOVED
Lynne Collins

Andrew married the woman he had always loved despite the knowledge that Sarah married him for reasons of her own. So much heartache could have been avoided if only he had known how vital it was to be loved.

ACCUSED NURSE
Jane Converse

Paula found herself accused of a crime which could cost her her job, her nurse's reputation, and even the man she loved, unless the truth came to light.

A GREAT DELIVERANCE
Elizabeth George

Into the web of old houses and secrets of Keldale Valley comes Scotland Yard Inspector Thomas Lynley and his assistant to solve a particularly savage murder.

'E' IS FOR EVIDENCE
Sue Grafton

Kinsey Millhone was bogged down on a warehouse fire claim. It came as something of a shock when she was accused of being on the take. She'd been set up. Now she had a new client — herself.

A FAMILY OUTING IN AFRICA
Charles Hampton and Janie Hampton

A tale of a young family's journey through Central Africa by bus, train, river boat, lorry, wooden bicycle and foot.

DEAD SPIT
Janet Edmonds

Government vet Linus Rintoul attempts to solve a mystery which plunges him into the esoteric world of pedigree dogs, murder and terrorism, and Crufts Dog Show proves to be far more exciting than he had bargained for . . .

A BARROW IN THE BROADWAY
Pamela Evans

Adopted by the Gordillo family, Rosie Goodson watched their business grow from a street barrow to a chain of supermarkets. But passion, bitterness and her unhappy marriage aliented her from them.

THE GOLD AND THE DROSS
Eleanor Farnes

Lorna found it hard to make ends meet for herself and her mother and then by chance she met two men — one a famous author and one a rich banker. But could she really expect to be happy with either man?

IN PALE BATTALIONS
Robert Goddard

Leonora Galloway has waited all her life to learn the truth about her father, slain on the Somme before she was born, the truth about the death of her mother and the mystery of an unsolved wartime murder.

A DREAM FOR TOMORROW
Grace Goodwin

In her new position as resident nurse at Coombe Magna, Karen Stevens has to bear the emnity of the beautiful Lisa, secretary to the doctor-on-call.

AFTER EMMA
Sheila Hocken

Following the author's previous auto-biographies — EMMA & I, and EMMA & Co., she relates more of the hilarious (and sometimes despairing) antics of her guide dogs.